Where's Sancho?
I

Don Quiett

A One Act Play and A Two Act Play

Inquires concerning all rights should be sent to P.O. Box 271,
Fuquay-Varina, North Carolina 27526

Published by Modern Aesthete

Cover artwork by Don Quiett
Cover design by Cari Corbett

Printed in the United States of America

First Edition

ISBN: 978-0-6151-4544-0

To Carol

TABLE OF CONTENTS

BEATING DRUM

Don Quiett

(One Act Play)

Acknowledgement

The writings of Cicero, Julius Caesar and other Roman authors were instrumental in this play's birth. However, David Sirota (<u>Hostile Takeover</u>), Norman Solomon (<u>War Made Easy</u>), Mark Miller (<u>Cruel and Unusual</u>) and Joe Conason (<u>It Can Happen Here</u>) unknowingly highlighted the similarities between then and now, making the play relevant for today's times.

ACT I

SETTING:

Living room/court yard of a Roman villa with pillars, Roman couches, fountain, vases, drapery etc. on 2/3rd of the stage; kitchen on the other 1/3rd of stage. There is one addition, however, to the décor, a circa 100 B.C. invention – a Likeness Box. Guests are gathering at Catalina's house to listen to a speech by Julius Caesar expounding on the need for military action in the northeast frontier and then farther east.

CHARACTERS: (*suggest all over act*)

Cicero – Great orator, lawyer, council, main problem was arrogance, self importance. Personal friend of Caesar. Died at Octavius (Augustus) and attorney's hands.

Cato – Fought Spartacus, popular with troops, one of them. Clerk of Treasury and knew how to run it. For a republic, not a dictatorship. Good soldier, bad politician.

Catalina – Pushed by Cicero's legal efforts, he moved from radical to revolutionary to pay debts, tried to overthrow Republic. Sulla's lieutenant, brave, loyal, blood thirsty.

Littlemus – Fictional spy from Caesar's vast spy network. Deformed, slightly hunched back.

Marcus – Freed slave, thus freeman; Roman subject.

Taro – Freeman cook. Happy, positive woman.

Lucius – Slave, hoping to become a freeman; general worker, helper in villa.

Vespa – Slave, woman works in kitchen under Taro's supervision.

Rufus – Old freeman, ex-slave, general handyman.

Pompeia – Julius Caesar's wife, after Cornelia, who was ruthless, former dictator Sulla's granddaughter.

Terentia – Cicero's wife from an influential, wealthy family.

CURTAIN RISES

1/3 kitchen side of stage light. Rest of stage dark.

MARCUS
(*Yelling, coming into kitchen*) Oysters! They want more oysters.

TARO
(*Cooking*) Ha! Sex, sex, sex, all they think about.

VESPA
(*Preparing the food*) Keeps them young, they say.

TARO
(*Laughing*) Didn't help you! Their <u>heads</u> are what they should worry about. Has Caesar started yet?

MARCUS
(*Resting, waiting, for the tray*) No, Taro.

TARO
Dark days ahead. The omens are here. Remember the Vestal's goat innards reading? Oh boy!

LUCIUS
(*Busy with pots, pans and wood and idly speaks*) For us!

They beat the drum and <u>we</u> die.

MARCUS
Right, but he has a good cause this time. Caesar does, Lucius. For sure.

TARO
In a word — NO —. Lying about how our life will be better — ya, well — good causes. Huh. Doesn't make me beat my drum fervently or otherwise.

RUFUS
(*Head slave, pacifying the help*) Now, now, none of that talk. Let's keep our jobs <u>and</u> our heads. Rome's rich must have their way. And profits. Us — survival. It is written.

VESPA
True, tongues can sink ships. And never know where the ears are that will send us to Neptune.

RUFUS
(*Angry, but practical*) Neptune's holy scales — <u>why</u> <u>worry</u>. One good fairy tale about us and — zap — it's <u>off</u> to the torture games.

MARCUS
Does, must say, it sounds like war again, to hear their verbal sparing.

LUCIUS
Praise Zeus' thunderbolts! Word gladiators, that's all they're good for. Words.

VESPA
You mean Jupiter. Don't you? (*Chuckling*)

LUCIUS

(*Angry*) Ha! Caesar trumps Jupiter now and should receive our sacrifices. You're right. And our prayers.

MARCUS

(*Shaking head*) Front line bait — that's all we'll be — human shields.

TARO

AAAA unn. We're not human to them. Oh, well. Hear anything real, while serving, Marcus?

MARCUS

(*Acts out peeling grapes*) Cato needs his grapes peeled. (*Laughs*) What's that about?

TARO

Thinks stops flatulence.

VESPA

Failed badly, I can tell you.

TARO

(*Laughing, then anxious and laughs again*) Saying sex and farts don't mix? Come on Marcus, give. Oh, first, where's big Flavious. Lazy giant pig, slave – need more wood for the oven. Can you picture him in the womb? Mount Vesuvius. (*Acts out huge belly, laughing*)

LUCIUS

(*Goes to get wood*) Jupiter, didn't you hear.

TARO

What?

LUCIUS

Unbelievable, but he's — dead! Stabbed. A dead gentle

giant.

TARO

Gods preserve. How?

LUCIUS

(*Acts out. Pretends to be each person*) Let me show
how I saw it. (*Prances around as does and says story*) The
giant door knocker echoes through the villa — again and
again and again, finally Catalina speaks: "Oh, precious
Aurelia could you get the door, my dear. Killed Flavious
this morn, so no door keeper." Then Aurelia says,
"Frightful nuisance." Catalina responds, "True, true.
But, the gall, looked me straight in the eye." Aurelia
declares, "What's Rome coming to?" Catalina ends,
"Better you don't know — skullduggery is afoot." (*Then
Lucius goes back to his normal behavior and stops acting
out*) But, do you believe it — that slave was no more
than a fly on the wall to be squashed. A hic-cup.

MARCUS

Skullduggery is right. (*Looks around to check no wrong
people hear*) I hear Catalina's debts are making him into
a revolutionary for solvency. Desires to take over Rome.
(*Looks secretive, whispers*) No other way he says.
Expanded all options.

TARO

Such big words. And you an ex-slave.

RUFUS

War, that's his tactic to get out of debt I've heard.

TARO

Civil War <u>and</u> major war together? Damn. Beating
drum. I bet poor slow Flavius was only confused. The
dear. What Gods should we do our devotions to for him?

LITTLEMUS

(B*ursts through side door*) Skullduggery, revolution, did I smell a whiff of these kitchen ingredients as I relieved myself in the privy?

MARCUS

Holy shit!

LITTLEMUS

No, just a leak.

VESPA

— a vegetable?

TARO

(*Laughing*) Beg pardon Master Littlemus, but what would a spy be here abouts for?

LITTLEMUS

Hush now, spies are bad things. I'm more a — a — finder — that's it, a finder. I find lost treasures, facts, people, plots, dead bodies — that's all.

RUFUS

Funny, always heard the Master say — spy.

LITTLEMUS

(*Eating something*) He would, but then has much hidden that needs found, he does.

RUFUS

You seem so nice, especially to us. Can't see why the Master and his friends fear you.

LUCIUS

(*Laughing*) Gets more out of <u>us</u> that way.

LITTLEMUS

(*Innocently says*) Fear me? Speak for yourself — me — I love all man.

VESPA

With that body, it's best to be plutonic.

LITTLEMUS

(*Preens himself*) Come my little one — most are intrigued by me.

MARCUS

(*Yells, jokingly*) Cut his oysters off.

VESPA

And wine.

LITTLEMUS

(*Acting arrogant*) Tut, tut – about this skullduggery now, I'm all ears.

TARO

(*Laughing*) Literally! Here, suck on this pickled melon rind. Rest your genitals and 'splain – is it War?

LITTLEMUS

(*Lovingly*) Your radiance pierces me.

MARCUS

Give! Or the spy rumor grows with our fertilizer. What's our fate?

LITTLEMUS

(*Uppity*) Picturesque, but OK. You drive a hard bargain. (*Looks in glass bottle or shiny pot as if crystal ball*) I see – yes I see a long journey – to the east – in your future.

LUCIUS
Shit! Persian gold, is that it? Will he ever get enough?

MARCUS
Settle, Lucius, the die is not cast.

LITTLEMUS
No, true, but let me inquire. Do you <u>want</u> the Gauls at your door again?

RUFUS
(*Angry*) Get off it Littlemus, that won't work again. That was Hispania's and Carthage's reasons. People won't buy it again! Will they?

LITTLEMUS
So, you do? Want them? Little Gauls everywhere.

MARCUS
Of course not, but that's a purple cow. Phony. Of long gone wars – death. Hades — they're domesticated, these Gauls are! Some even work, guard, the Palazzo estate here.

LITTLEMUS
(*Laughing*) Yes, but who are the next little Gauls — look to the east.

VESPA
(*Said slowly in a depressed tone*) Boom — boom — boom – where's my drum.

LITTLEMUS
(*Nonchalantly*) Stopping them there is Caesar's wish. That's all. So, they are not at our gates.

TARO

(*Pondering*) That chance is zilch. Not worth <u>one</u> life. They can't even get here. Besides, more to be concerned with — like <u>citizens</u> breaking down the gates or, just plain stealing them. (*Laughs*)

LITTLEMUS

Then, you don't remember Hannibal?

TARO

(*Laughing, while cooking*) Hades, that was 2-300 years ago. Things have changed.

LITTLEMUS

Sleepless nights, it gives Caesar. Worry of a new Hannibal. His appetite fails with worry.

LUCIUS

Gods don't need to eat.

LITTLEMUS

I'll tell the Great One. He loves praise.

MARCUS

(*Worrying voice*) Remember to whom we speak.

LUCIUS

(*Serious, fearful*) Jupiter! Please don't report me. I take it back. Bad joke. Pals, Littlemus?

LITTLEMUS

Blasphemy, is that your response to Caesar's fatherly protection of his people? Come now, Gaul, Hannibal, Celts did happen. They <u>must</u> be stopped. Better there than here.

CICERO

(*Pokes head in kitchen door*) Did I hear the Persians are coming? Littlemus you deceiver, thought I heard you. What are you eating?

LITTLEMUS

Cicero, Your Largeness, have one, they're great. Pickled rinds.

CICERO

So, you've heard the rumors too, even in this kitchen dungeon.

MARCUS

What, Cicero?

CICERO

He plays dumb better than you, Littlemus. Maybe he's in the wrong profession.

LITTLEMUS

What are your rumors, oh Glutinous One? These stuffed figs with almonds covered in honey are delectable.

CICERO

(*Taking food and chewing exaggeratingly*) Fortunately, I'm a wise man, not a bully. So, I'll not be pricked by your barbs.

MARCUS

Stop the oysters!

CICERO

Pricked, not prick, you fool. Tasty figs though. Let's stay in the kitchen tonight and sample the goodies, skip the "party."

MARCUS

Your weight, master, is not trivial. Seems a bad idea –
you — kitchen.

LITTLEMUS

Yes, Your Enorm —

CICERO

Stop it! My togas are baggy, I lose weight.

LITTLEMUS

More guests, do I hear? Should we retreat from this
kitchen oasis? Cicero?

CICERO

Yes, yes, yes — never. Stomachs — that's what a soldier
fights on.

LITTLEMUS

Hum — cook's a genius — mullet with piquant sauce, fat
thrushes, wild boar and truffles.

CICERO

(*Chewing, speaking meticulously*) Or is it peacock?
Well, Littlemus, do you buy this unpatriotic line we're
tossed? Speak against this new war and you'll be
skewered with the arrows of unpatriotism. Anti-Caesar.

LITTLEMUS

(*Whispering*) Quiet! Apollo's holy arrows. Keep your
voice down.

CICERO

Well?

LITTLEMUS

(*Said dejectedly*) Popular opposition is not welcome.

Granted. Hard to argue with a God in waiting.

TARO
Gossip has it, we're to unite <u>for peace</u>. Give the enemy, whoever that may be, no false hope. War is peace.

LUCIUS
Right. We citizens must <u>unite against defeat</u>.

CICERO
Sweet Aphrodites, Caesar's good. Far greater than <u>my</u> oratory abilities.

VESPA
Of course, Master. He's Caesar. God.

CICERO
Yes, yes, yes — no. Who <u>else</u> could convince the masses to die for country, not for the pleasure of destroying others, and without personal gain.

LITTLEMUS
(*Mockingly*) Ya, the moral high road. Rome is all.

CICERO
Self deception cries out.

RUFUS
I'd die to protect Rome. Our way of life. Best in the world. You speak treason!

CICERO
No. My friendly Rufus, no. We only philosophize on the ways of man — his survival — his propaganda.

RUFUS
Oh — ok.

LUCIUS

(*Looks confused*) Says Caesar is the greatest purveyor of violence in the world today. And, face it, Catalina knows violence.

TARO

Nonsense, you would be slave. Caesar is — properly masculine. He must hold up citizen morale, make us feel 'see-cure'.

LUCIUS

Yea, don't want some dumb Greek or Turk walking all over us. Do you? Peace through strength. That's our Caesar.

CICERO

(*Whispers*) Jupiter, Littlemus, is there hope? Their brains seem to have been cleansed of reason.

MARCUS

(*Scratches head, thinking*) What do they call it when you see something a second time when you didn't really see it the first time?

TARO

Weird.

MARCUS

No, no, this is just like the Gallic War, even though I wasn't there.

CICERO

See what you mean. Sulla or someone said, 'we need this war for security.' Most, more than half the populace of freemen said — '<u>no</u> we don't.'

LITTLEMUS
Ya, then Sulla said, (*Acts imperial*) "That 'no' attitude"
sends the wrong message to our troops, our enemies.

MARCUS
Crucifixions is what I saw, beheadings.

LITTLEMUS
Funny how 100% of our citizens then agreed with our
leader – amazing.

MARCUS
So much for aid and comfort to the enemy. Gaul was
doomed.

CICERO
Well put, Marcus. I may use that.

MARCUS
What don't you use? Steal?

VESPA
The war must be promoted, undertaken. Caesar would
not lie. We must defend ourselves.

CICERO
From the mouths of babes.

MARCUS
How successful was Antony's peace trip?

CICERO
I fear it only short circuits genuine debate. Done deal
before Antony went.

LITTLEMUS
Right there, Your Enormousness. Senate babbled, agreed,

but debate? No. Just words. Up is down, white is black.
Crimson herrings. Yet, citizens think great wisdom
arrived at. Consensus.

CICERO
Conformity! Conformity of thought, enforced conformity
is demanded by the Great One. The uniform consensus
of one. Conformity to war. The beating drum.

MARCUS
Your masters, you must get back. Antony enters. Thank
you for the entertainment.

*Lights on the kitchen, slave, third of stage go dark as Cicero and
Littlemus pass through door way into the proper residence side.
Lights up some on the 2/3 side with spot light on main speakers.
Alternate between all light and spot light in this section of house
as appropriate. Initial spot light focus is on Cato greeting
Catalina. Antony is off to side silent, stoic and glowing.*

CATALINA
Hail the Great One. Greetings Cato. How went the
forum today?

CATO
Stinking – our sewer works are atrocious – need reformed.
Speaking of sewers, I didn't know Cicero would be here.
<u>Antony</u>!

CATALINA
(*To change subject*) The cost! Jupiter's lightening bolts
that would empty the treasury. Just for sewers!

CATO
Treasury's already empty. All these damn conflicts.
Only one getting rich from these wars is Caesar. With
his taxes.

CATALINA

And by the confiscation of property from those seen
committing heresy in Caesar's eyes. But to the point.
Better you move your house higher up the hill to escape
the sultry air, I'd say. Stop complaining. Safer.

Pompeia comes over.

CATO

(*Whispers to Catalina*) Careful now, here comes Caesar's
Prima Vera spy. (*Greets women*) Pompeia, how is
Caesar's wife this fine eve?

POMPEIA

Cut the crap. What are you two plotting? My husband's
job?

CATO

Sewers. We need new ones. Cleaner.

POMPEIA

Metaphors! So, you are plotting – in metaphors.

CATALINA

(*Laughing*) Ha, ha, ha. Your wit, Pompeia, makes you
priceless, even more priceless than Our Divine One.

POMPEIA

Flattery won't work, Catalina. You still must pay back
your Egyptian plunder.

CATALINA

(*Quickly changes subject*) Cato, do you know Caesar's
topic tonight?

POMPEIA

Ha! Servilia, Cato's half sister and Caesar's whatever and

Brutus mother, would never tell Cato the truth. His stoic doctrines — "be true to oneself regardless of outside forces" — makes him a poor confidant.

CATALINA

Could he be beating the drum? — Again?

POMPEIA

Naughty, naughty.

CATO

Well, he does believe military action prevents all manor of calamity.

CATALINA

The news postings on the forum walls have been percolating; spouting war's needed, more and more. Yes, ever increasing.

CATO

Even senators are infected with this propaganda. Peace isn't won, it's taken. Free thought is overrated.

POMPEIA

The Great One will not bite off more than his military can chew. Be assured. I'd watch my words Cato.

CATALINA

Speaking of chewed, try the honeyed shrimp. Or honeyed bread. Honey's our food theme tonight.

POMPEIA

Terentia, is that her? Cato, you are becoming political, if Cicero's here, and you still came. I knew you were more than a warrior. Spartacus knew. (*Calls out and leaves*) Terentia!

Work on lighting and what comes on and off depending on who speaks for emphasis and illusion of a large room. Slave 1/3 still dark.

CATO

(*To Cicero*) Your wife and Caesar's are more friendly than usual I see.

CICERO

Aren't marriages wonderful? My daughter and Caesar's aide. Pompey and Caesar's daughter. Just one big happy family.

CATALINA

You threaten us?

CICERO

(*Surprised*) Sweet Apollo, no. So, what's Caesar's speech to be on, on that infernal LIKENESS Box tonight?

CATO

Gods know. How's that box work, anyway? Seems like Caesar's eyes are everywhere. Watching. Watching, watching.

CATALINA

If nothing to hide, why fear it?

CICERO

But who wants to live that way, even if nothing to fear. Besides, told it only goes one way. Out. Information can't go into it.

CATO

Who really knows?

CATALINA

Rumor has it, Caesar said it came direct from Jupiter himself, as a gift, during one of their meetings.

CATO

Holy balls! They're the same now, aren't they?

CATALINA

(*Said in conspiratory tone*) Shushhh. Blasphemy you fool. Get your head removed. Thank the Gods it only goes one way.

CICERO

Me, I think there's more in that dark night void with twinkling lights than just Jupiter.

CATALINA

Holy togas! Shut-up.

CATO

Catalina's right, or the vestals might torch your scrotum with such speaking.

CICERO

(*Said pouting like*) Well, there is more! Jupiter's not all — ask his wife.

CATO AND CATALINA

Huh?

CICERO

Truly where <u>did</u> that LIKENESS BOX come from? It will ruin our civilization.

CATO

Come now. The speech — what drum does he beat tonight?

Littlemus comes to the group. Others wandering around chit-chatting and eating.

LITTLEMUS
The honeyed grass or whatever is delicious. So, fess up, what conspiracy does this group chew on?

CICERO
Funny. We pontificate on the congruity, the fastidiousness, the origin, the ways of — the Box?

LITTLEMUS
(*Shrugs back as if doesn't believe them*) Right. Nature's wonder. I suppose.

CATO
Facts, especially from Caesar's flunkies, are not often factual. Thoughts, oh Littlemus?

LITTLEMUS
Me? I know nothing.

CATALINA
If Caesar wants a war, he'll get one.

LITTLEMUS
Beyond me. I don't know his drum beat.

CICERO
Some spy. Is not Vercingotrix (*said –bur-sing-tor-rec*), or Boudicca on the move again?

LITTLEMUS
Distant rumbles do grow. I hear Julius say, I guess.

CICERO
Guess?

LITTLEMUS

He fears another Hannibal, he says. An attack on Rome
proper over the Alps, he says. He only wants to safe
guard the citizens — he says.

CATO

Sounds like a drum beat to war to me!

CATALINA

(*Plotting with anger, whispery voice*) Rumor again, but
didn't he secretly send aids to Hispania and Persia to
assess the threat of hostilities? Perception management, I
heard him call it.

CATO

Rumors shit! The notices are posted everywhere for
citizen consumption. What secret?

CICERO

(*Flippant*) Does seem from the poster campaign the
conclusions of a torrid debate on Rome's well being have
been undertaken when in reality, no such debate has
occurred. I hear the drum, too.

LITTLEMUS

Come, come. Caesar only wants <u>social</u> justice for all
people <u>in distant</u> lands. Just <u>like Rome's</u>. Popular
revolution is all. Republican senates for <u>all</u> mankind he
wants.

CATALINA

Right! Social justice my feces of the bull. To line his
pockets! All he wants.

LITTLEMUS

And not yours?

CATALINA

I hope. So, who's our evil man this time?

LITTLEMUS

Only the Gods know.

CATO

Part of the drum beat says — the <u>Great One</u> wasn't
getting tough enough, fast enough.

CICERO

(*Laughing*) That's priceless. I couldn't even defend that
with <u>my</u> great oratory. Posters say citizens say — not
tough enough — yet citizens don't know against whom
yet. Priceless, only Caesar.

LITTLEMUS

His Generals — they must of leaked. Secret information
they have, you don't. They know, you don't. Have a
plan, only waiting for the right time. You don't know it.

CICERO

Secret! Even from the Senate? No debate?

CATO

Yep — the new way.

CATALINA

Way to sell war, without drawing attention to it.

CICERO

(*Shakes head with smirk*) What wondrous times we live
in. Secrets will be our down fall — I swear.

LITTLEMUS

Cicero take care. Trust me, a truly <u>evil</u> <u>man</u> lurks outside
our walls. Secrecy to the last — a must. Our open

society requires such secrecy.

CICERO

(*Says to the side*) Outrageous.

LITTLEMUS

What?

CICERO

(*Humorously*) Ostentatious — I said — this food is. Let us partake.

LITTLEMUS

Trust Caesar, Cicero. This next war will be a good war, as good as it can be.

CICERO

Telling me it's necessary, justified, righteous, worth any sorrow?

LITTLEMUS

Would I lie? Better, would Caesar? He loves the people. He is their best friend. Never lies to them.

Pompeia and Terentia come over to the group. Littlemus leaves. Lighting changes appropriately.

POMPEIA

Break it up, come on, break it up, enough. The food spoils.

TERENTIA

(*Excited, laughing*) True, but Pompeia tells of other coming spoils.

POMPEIA

Shusshh!

TERENTIA

Cicero, Cato and Catalina, our money problems will be over soon.

CATALINA

How so?

POMPEIA

Terentia, that was <u>our secret!</u>

TERENTIA

Ooohh! My mouth runs away with joy. Sorry Pompeia.

CATALINA

Well?

POMPEIA

<u>Can</u> see why you have <u>no</u> money Catelina, if you can't see this one. And <u>you</u> want to lead a country!

CATALINA

Ok, ok, conquered territory means more taxes to collect. That doesn't help me!

CICERO

Listen Catalina, in a word — grain.

CATALINA

What?

CATO

Stupid! Think! In Egypt, you made money; you lost money — on what?

CATALINA

(*Said weakly*) Grain??

CICERO

Gaul, Persia — think — number one product — grain!
Get it?

POMPEIA

We corner the market after the war and we are hailed as
benevolent conquers — grain, grain, grain everywhere,
and it's ours. Humongous profits.

CATO

War is not terror and death for us: it's profits! Fool!

POMPEIA

Tribunes, freemen, slaves win the wars. Civilize the
barbarous conquered. And we — we nobles win the
market place.

CICERO

This drum beat will make us humongously wealthy? War
commerce, along with war spoils!

TERENTES

Ends our servant problem too. And stops the terrible
gossip.

CATALINA

Gossip? Mean like the radical's dribble of how the
nobleman's, old families', wealth grows more than that of
Rome's citizens? Unfair claim.

POMPEIA

Right, he must stem this faulty perception about us. We
don't loaf, we are the struggling noble rich. We only reap
what our hard work sows. Where would the citizens be
without us?

CATALINA

(*Late realization*) Neptune's holy britches, <u>the profits</u>!
Banking, property sales, tourism for <u>our</u> class. The
possibilities are endless.

CATO

(*Said light heartedly*) Me thinks he's getting it. War is
good! Beat that drum, Catalina. Beat it.

CICERO

(*Said in slow flat depressed tone*) War is good — yaaa —
for us noblemen — anyway. Where's that honeyed
shrimp?

CATO

I hear Caesar wants to strengthen his grip on the Empire
only for its own good, so this War beat. Boom. Boom.
Boom.

CATALINA

War's war. Big deal. Spoils is our goal. Yes, spoils!

CATO

How did you get this far, Catalina? No wonder you're
broke. Think man. Think!

CATALINA

I'm a General. Fighter. Spoils of war are my prize. Your
point?

CATO

Shoes man! Shoes!

CATALINA

What? Thought it was grain, plunder.

POMPEIA
The War machine is greased with shoes, swords, shields, coats, spears. We supply that grease! At engorged prices! (*Laughs*) Prices suitable for war time that is.

TERENTIA
And the great, wonderful caring Caesar claims he only wants 5% of our profits this time. Get it, yet Catalina?

CICERO
And that's a 5% profit <u>above</u> and <u>beyond</u> Caesar's normal financial spoils of war prizes represented with taxes, free shipping, gold transactions, gems, humans etc, etc, etc. Rome's treasure chest should be bulging at the seams — bursting.

CATALINA
This is true? There's money to be made? Profit before and during, not only after the clashes. Jupiter!

TERENTIA
Look at his face (*Laughs*). High finance dawns in Catalina.

CATO
Caesar'll buy enough allies with this 5% scheme, to guarantee adequate support for his world — known and unknown — conquest.

CICERO
Dreaming big was never his flaw. Must be <u>with</u> him <u>or</u> against him. No other choice, if that's a choice. Profits, profits: war should be about <u>more</u>, it would seem.

POMPEIA
Ha! There is no more. Profits are the apex. Why have a war if no profits?

TERENTIA

War is good. Yes it is. (*Holds up pearls around her neck*)

CATO

Good for something. I guess. War is peace.

CICERO

Aaaahhh, Littlemus, may I have a word?

Cicero, joined by spy Littlemus, goes to the kitchen. Nobles side darkens, kitchen lights up again.

CICERO

I wither. Where's some food? Artemus save me from the drunken gluttons in the other room.

MARCUS

Come, come a week without food would suit you, oh, Your Immenseness, orator Cissy. And leave more air for us.

CICERO

(*Laughing*) I could have your head, Marcus. Respect? I get none.

LITTLEMUS

We should have stayed here. What bullocks they are in there.

VESPA

(*Laughing*) Bullocks? Are we into oysters again? Huh?

LITTLEMUS

(*Said disgustedly*) Levity, in a time of drum beating? War? Great!

LUCUS

You're not serious, sir. Not another one. We just

finished one. Hispania. Remember last year? Surely Caesar beats a different drum.

TARO
Hear Caesar doesn't want to confuse us. So his speech tonight. Drum beat.

VESPA
Ya. Heard his spies say overwhelming evidence Vercingotrix (pronounced BUR- SINC-TOR-REC) is trying to join up with that Persian evil one. To destroy us.

RUFUS
Right. Truly there is a <u>sinister nexus</u> to murder us all.

LITTLEMUS
(*Whispers to Cicero*) I missed that one.

CICERO
Some spy!, you are Littlemus.

TARO
Ya, ya. No hoax. Long established ties. Overwhelming evidence – a connection between Gaul and Persia.

RUFUS
Caesar needs us! We must protect ourselves. For sure. Protect <u>our</u> Rome!

CICERO
(*Whispers to Littlemus*) Damn. Those poster campaigns seem to be more potent then I perceived.

LITTLEMUS
Don't underestimate the masses. Caesar truly <u>has them</u> wanting him to beat the drum.

CICERO

(*Said slowly and sarcastically*) Boom — boom.

TARO

Some stuffed figs? Stuffed with chopped almonds and
smothered in a honey basting? Or something else to eat?
Peeled grapes?

All help laugh.

LITTLEMUS

(*Ignores servants*) Marcus, you hear Caesar, read his
posters, why do you <u>want</u> war?

MARCUS

Can't say I do, but don't want to die.

LITTLEMUS

And you, Lucius?

LUCIUS

Seems best if we corner the violence in the world — that
way guarantee our safety.

CICERO

Well put Lucius. To be — so violent the rest of the
world runs from us — or not to be. That does seem the
question.

MARCUS

No, no. We all want peace, even Caesar. It's just that
it's not that simple.

TARO

Protective stupidity — that's what I call it.

LITTLEMUS

Profound.

TARO

(*Laughing*) Naw. Not him. Read it on a privy wall. Had to be written by a guy, a prophet or something though.

VESPA

Sounds to me like Caesar's making it not such a big deal. This war stuff.

LUCIUS

I agree — Caesar says foes are not foes and their masses will meet us with open arms, as friends, wreath us in flowers. We'll free them from their oppressor.

LITTLEMUS

(*Whispers to Cicero*) Great Neptune, Caesar's propaganda is good. Really good!

CICERO

Eloquent you are little man.

VESPA

Well, if you ask me — us against "The World" is not a good thing, or friendly.

TARO

Nor makes much common sense.

VESPA

Ha! Common sense? Defined as — obtuse, twisted thinking of the world of men! I wouldn't bet my best tunic on it. Common sense, some myth! War — the greatest myth.

MARCUS

(*Thinking out loud attitude*) But, if we free them, all freemen can live in harmony? Isn't that a truism?

LITTLEMUS

Would the door keeper here agree? I mean ex-keeper.

LUCIUS

That was different. Flavious had not bought or earned his free status yet. And certainly he was not a plebian or of the subject people.

CICERO

I must think on that statement a moment. Obvious flaw somewhere in there.

TARO

It's only common sense — for a man, anyway.

LITTLEMUS

Well, take only the freemen then, common man.

VESPA

Seems one's free only when it's advantageous to the rich patrician class. But that's woman's common sense.

LUCIUS

Watch it Vespa, ears are here. Don't want reported.

LITTLEMUS

Relax. I'm off duty.

MARCUS

What's the question, again?

LITTLEMUS

Why do you want war?

MARCUS

Not up to me. Our leaders know best.

CICERO

But there are more of you than anyone, that makes you common. Plentiful. Should not <u>common</u> man's — <u>common</u> sense — decide his destiny?

LUCIUS

(*Laughing*) Get out.

MARCUS

Right. Otherwise the masses would never fight. No wars. We would opt to keep our arms and legs. Face it, Caesar's wars never improve our plight, only worsen it.

CICERO

The common man speaks. Yet, Caesar's words create believable absurdities with its resultant injustices <u>and</u> we declare such things good.

LITTLEMUS

You are wordy, <u>or</u> is it from the <u>privy</u> too?

CICERO

No, the future speaking to me.

Departs to other room, lights go out in the kitchen and then go on in nobleman's side. Spot light on Cicero and Littlemus as they leave.

LITTLEMUS

We better get back.

CICERO

Right. Don't want you to miss any rich spy stuff.

CATALINA

What he says maybe true. But it seems it's not the complete story. He prevaricates. Right Cicero? Would you not say that?

CICERO

(*Humorously*) Prevaricate? Not sure of its meaning in the context.

CATALINA

Littlemus?

LITTLEMUS

I know nothing.

CATALINA

Plain as day. The narrow view is: Caesar touts barbarian atrocities must stop. But in a wider view, hard to miss the hypocrisy and manipulation.

LITTLEMUS

I would change the subject Catalina. Someone might take it you side with the enemy.

CATALINA

Only the enemy's innocent.

CATO

There are no innocent in war!

CICERO

(*Sarcastically*) Yes, women, children and the aged present a clear and present danger. Well, at least they provide a profit!

CATALINA

Yes, profit. I grasp your meaning. Right. Littlemus,

thank you. I cage my idealistic thoughts and feed them to the lions.

LITTLEMUS

Now, wasn't that easy?

CICERO

Littlemus, you are a devil.

POMPEIA

(*Coming over with Terentia*) Come now citizens. You weasels must firm your backbone. War is easy. Quit fretting. Easy as pie.

CICERO

Spoken like a true elitist.

POMPEIA

Careful, Cicero. Your consular position is not that secure. One whisper in the right ear and it's banishment, back to Greece.

CICERO

I bow to your wishes.

POMPEIA

You better. Fat One.

CICERO

I was only suggesting —

POMPEIA

I wouldn't.

CICERO

— that distance, privilege and illusion create a sense of ease about war.

POMPEIA

(*Ponders*) Not bad. I'll hold my whisper. <u>For now</u>.

LITTLEMUS

The kitchen slaves, freemen, however, could probable see Cicero's point. Especially if count arms and legs.

POMPEIA

What? You dottie old cripple.

LITTLEMUS

Only purveying the sense of folly at putting easy and war in the same sentence.

POMPEIA

(*Jesters hand flip under chin*) Purvey this, you cuckold.

TERENTIA

Come now, think on it. The money? I like and understand the money part of war, oh do I ever. (*Shows off jewels and acts flighty*) But how do you get these beasts to fight over and over and over again? Confuses me.

POMPEIA

Not hard — your confusion. Stick to the oysters and bed rooms Terentia. Don't bruise your brain with thoughts.

LITTLEMUS

A poignant observation though.

POMPEIA

Piss off little guy. Caesar speaks — they obey. Like this Terentia — Caesar says fight – fighters say OK. Caesar says jump – soldiers say how high. Caesar says charge — soldiers run ahead. Get it? Orders from the Supreme Being must be followed.

CATO

In essence Pompeia, you're right. But will you win with such men? Rarely. Caesar knows. Probably why the speech.

CATALINA

Has done it before. Even soldiers need a cause, not just orders.

LITTLEMUS

Enemies. Enemies, we have so many. Why do you think that is?

CATO

With faces like Veringotrex or Boudicca, what do you expect? Especially, displayed at the end of a spike.
(*Laughs nastily*)

CICERO

Sweet Cato. The simpleton. Listen to the Likeness Box's Caesar: "We are being attacked!" — True? Littlemus? Is it?

LITTLEMUS

No.

CICERO

No! So why? Why this charade? Pompeia? Cato? ?

All shake heads, act like don't know.

CICERO

Well, a good leader knows, as does Caesar, for good fighting men who will do your bidding, they have to believe they are under threat. House fear in their bodies.

LITTLEMUS
Right on there, oh Enormous One. Fear. Caesar's secret weapon. Soldiers must fear for their women and children.

CICERO
Fear loss of their life style.

LITTLEMUS
Loss of freedom, their wealth. Fear needs a face and why so many enemies we have. Fear. Fear. Fear.

CICERO
Correctamundo. Then they fight with passion. A victorious passion. Yes, Caesar knows. Another beating drum.

POMPEIA
So, fear must back up orders? I can buy that, I like fear – in others.

LITTLEMUS
All who speak against Caesar's will <u>must</u> be denounced.

CICERO
(*Laughing*) Notice any forum pacifists? Negotiators for peace? If did, it was not for long.

LITTLEMUS
Right again, Pudgy One. Any declared lack of patriotism exposes the country to <u>great danger</u>. To the hanging tree with them.

CATO
Altruism: Subject people must be resolved. And back the "Supreme One" — <u>no matter what.</u> Thus, Caesar's speech — we are under threat, being attacked, and

pacifism will not work.

CICERO
A time honored slogan. Yes indeed.

CATO
As Jupiter says — to dupe the masses, have many
enemies.

LITTLEMUS
Enemies, a crucial need. A must, as a matter of fact.
And with real faces to hate.

CICERO
No enemies, no wars, no profits.

TERENTIA
Oh, forget it. Who cares? I'm always confused anyway.
So, let's talk about money again. Profits. War profits.
My favorite subject.

All activity ceases, all are quiet, serious and stare at Terentia.

LITTLEMUS
(*Breaks silence*) Caesar does have a point though, about a
new kind of war profit.

CICERO
(*Looks stunned*) Where'd that come from? Oh, well
enlighten us, oh Tiny One.

CATO
You're not talking about that "arm the Gauls" idiocy, are
you?

CATALINA
Ha! Arm our enemy! Jupiter's roses.

POMPEIA
Caesar's plan deserves more respect.

CATO
Sorry, your Greatness. It's just that I've killed so many Gauls that re-arming them seems a fantasy. Beyond me.

POMPEIA
That's why Caesar is Caesar, the Omnipotent One.

LITTLEMUS
Back to old Terra Firma folks. Basically, by arming our so-called enemies —

CATALINA
So — called. Ha!

LITTLEMUS
— we encourage Gauls to fight Gauls, Persians to fight Persians, Britons — Britons.

CATO
Which frees up our troops? To fight elsewhere?

LITTLEMUS
Or to not fight at all. More importantly, it allows us to control these barbarians by a proxy emperorship.

CATO
Get out. No way. That's really stupid.

CICERO
As I see it, if the price is right and we buy enough Barbarian chieftains we maintain imperial control while the occupied become their own occupiers, loyal to us.

LITTLEMUS

Brilliant! Brilliant! Don't know why they say you're so
dumb.

CATALINA

Is that possible? The occupied,
occupying themselves?

CATO

Right! Oh Catalina, you are as stupid as a slave.

LITTLEMUS

For the right price they can. Think man!

CATALINA

But it would never last.

LITTLEMUS

That's where Caesar's cunning plan comes in. And is
profitable for us to boot. True Empire security. Rome
land security. Romanization.

CICERO

I'm all ears. Logic, reason is set back beyond Socrates'
time. Aristotle's grave erupts like a volcano.

CATO

I don't get this. We beat the shit out of the Barbarians.
They happily do our bidding and oppress the locals. We
profit, they eat crap — war is hell. Isn't it?

LITTLEMUS

On target! Picture this, the Barbarians work with us,
become part of our economy, gain profit, thus war
becomes obsolete. Impossible. Caesar's long range
vision.

CATO

Jupiter's, Zeus's, Apollo's — somebody's holy toga
catches fire. Why? Why? Why? Why would they do it?

LITTLEMUS

(*Speaks teacher like*) Barbarian chieftains like profit too.
Greed works miracles. Not fighting is in their own best
interests now. OK, impossible maybe too big a word. But
close.

CATALINA

Kill a calf — check Caesar's sanity.

LITTLEMUS

Wait gentlemen. Think!

POMPEIA

Think? OK. Commerce. All this would foster
commerce. Ya, OK. Investments. No war, yet we profit
like there is a war. Is that the point?

LITTLEMUS

You smell virgin-hood again.

POMPEIA

Ha, ha, ha! You are a fart.

CATO

But will the masses stand for this? Won't they revolt?

LITTLEMUS

Not likely. Think of it! War benefits special interests.

CATO

Ya, but you have to beat someone.

LITTLEMUS

Not necessarily; in these modern times.

CICERO

The reverie clears. Economic reform, free trade, so to speak, dawns.

LITTLEMUS

You always were quick.

CATALINA

I'm not.

POMPEIA

Even I see it.

CATALINA

Well!

POMPEIA

Money, profits, gigantic! Lucrative investments can reach to Jupiter. Take your concrete.

CATALINA

(*Weakly*) My new brick glue?

POMPEIA

Correct. With this idiocy, you can sell it safely, prodigiously from the Britons to Persia. You, only you, corner the market. Otherwise there would be war. And nobody, at least no leaders anyway, wants war.

CICERO

Less profit in war now for them. So go along to get along. Commerce flies like Icarus.

LITTLEMUS
Cunning! Caesar's plan to make the barbarians into mini "us"es will make for safe commerce. Yet, the reality will be that they will not be much beyond slaves for Rome.

CATO
No more war. Cleaver, is it not? Romanization, par excellence.

CATALINA
(*Said as if questioning self*) So, the only concrete the world can buy is from me. To do this, we arm the Gauls, Britons, Persians who <u>occupy</u> their <u>own</u> countries for us, thinking they're practicing free will. Granted their leaders do this for a small reward, but one which is <u>big</u> to them. Thus we profit like it's war, but there is no war. Right?

LITTLEMUS
Got it!

CATALINA
Genius! Temples, civilization wide, built to the heavens, due to <u>my</u> concrete. Big!

CATO
(*Pulls aside, spot light only them*) Listen, we could do this on our own. Who needs Caesar?

CATALINA
(*Ponders*) Right. My revolt truly begins now. With <u>me</u>. My Egyptian debts resolved. Caesar's in my line of sight. The Gods are good.

CATO
Excellent. Our soldiering <u>should</u> have been worth more than we've gotten to date. Right Catalina? Caesar has

done us wrong.

CATALINA

True.

All stage lights up for patricians.

TERENTIA

(*Walks up to them*) You guys can talk and talk, but <u>do</u> you realize the Likeness Box's potential?

CATO

Who cares?

TERENTIA

Gladiator games without the heat and sun! Jupiter, how great that would be.

CATALINA

(*Pondering*) Spectators of comfort. Stay in your own villa and watch. It is a concept of merit.

POMPEIA

Frightening. What minds I have to endure, always so serious. Ha, ha, ha. You should soar up with the Gods, Terentia.

CICERO

(*Acting lawyer summation*) It seems, full circle we've come. I picture the mosaic now.

CATALINA

I didn't know you were an artist, Cicero.

CATO

The Gods, Catalina! Metaphors. Ever hear of them?

CATALINA

Huh

CICERO

Anyway, our enemies are to be domesticated, sold arms, have natural resources extracted to enrich Rome's brave souls via commerce with politically connected firms to benefit Caesar's interests.

CATO

Damn right. That's where war profits without war comes in.

CICERO

(*Holds head*) Mind boggling.

Cicero and Littlemus walk away from group with spot light on them.

LITTLEMUS

Finders do have a value. Admit it Cicero. Come on. Say it.

CICERO

As long as the people get no whiff of their leader's doings, all might work. And they will stink. The leader's doings, that is.

LITTLEMUS

The trick is to make sure the yoke does not strangle the ox.

CICERO

Which ox?

LITTLEMUS

Good point. Both.

CICERO

The people's yoke should be of little trouble. So you lose a few, big deal. But the barbarian leaders? They require a conjuror.

LITTLEMUS

Correct. Your Hugeness. Their subjugation has pitfalls. Greed primarily, but more importantly their ability as <u>actors</u>.

CICERO

Actors?

LITTLEMUS

Actors who can convince the masses they have the interests of <u>their</u> society at heart. Tricky that is.

CICERO

Romanization. Is that the word for today's financial world? Commerce — <u>ill</u> — a — zation — or is that the new word for war? Worldalization! Nobility-wise?

LITTLEMUS

It's not a <u>fighting</u> war, <u>is</u> all I know.

CICERO

As long as the leaders stay bought and the occupied are kept so, unknowingly. Otherwise let the rumble begin.

LITTLEMUS

Pessimist.

CATO

(*Comes over acting confused, worried*) Is this forged, or whatever, cooperation practical?

CICERO

(*Acts melodramatic*) Archimedes is called for! Economic geometry even! Equations for stark materialism bloom. God what a vision.

CATO

Harsh, Cicero. Kinda harsh. You might, with a little effort, might have made a good soldier with that thinking.

LITTLEMUS

Nations are out dated. Face it. That's Caesar's goal. Trade among nations will be gone. No nations. The marketplace will be one. And as a result — no war.

CICERO

And, I bet, this <u>one</u> marketplace where <u>free trade</u> abounds will be controlled by — Rome. Or more precisely — its leaders. Power brokers. Concrete makers.

LITTLEMUS

Now you've found the true Apian Way, Cicero.

CICERO

You need a linguist or some such. I fear — free — is other than what it use to be.

LITTLEMUS

Technical, technical. That may work for a trial defense, but of little value in commerce.

CATO

Or of value for the end of war forever.

CICERO

Let me play Socrates to your Aristotle with questions.

CATO

Give it a break, Cicero. Put it to bed. One who fights
the ways of Caesar may risk being labeled a traitor.

LITTLEMUS

To what end? Answer that before Cato banishes you to
your beloved Greece.

CICERO

Who knows? First question, is not a restriction of
freedoms for the greater majority of people required?

LITTLEMUS

If a group pursues its private advantage, yes.

CICERO

Must the political process be stifled, corrupted?

CATO

Sure! Daft! Why else make occupiers out of the
occupied through its leaders?

CICERO

Will state powers manage markets for private benefit?

CATO

Damn right. Otherwise, what's the point? Spoils to the
conquerors and all that rot.

CICERO

Will there be a self-destructive nature to this process?

CATO

(*Hesitantly*) No. Definitively no. No to whatever you
mean.

CICERO

(*Pats Cato on head*) This maybe hard Cato, pay close attention.

CATO

Piss off. Lawyers!

CICERO

You plan to undermine present economic balance. So what guidepost, markers, are to be used to evaluate said undermining?

CATO

(*Laughing*) Go on! You've been eating too much pheasant.

CICERO

Possibly, but we've known decades of financial security in Rome. What's the effect of this new approach to be? How monitor?

CATO

Stupid questions. Don't get it. You're making problems where there are none.

LITTLEMUS

Cato, does have a point.

CICERO

When is the time right for this new program for security without the rules of the past?

LITTLEMUS

Now, of course.

CICERO

What is the endpoint?

LITTLEMUS

Superfluous question. There is none. The <u>means</u> is important. For the nobles anyway, not the masses. We must strive for the perfection of the means. Not a specific end. The <u>how</u>, not the <u>what</u>!

CICERO

(*Hold arms up, then slaps side of hips*) I rest my case. I find this all brittle. Success, ultimate success, depends on mass approval and yet, mass appeal is purposely shunned.

CATO

(*Angrily*) You're cracked. We have the power, do what want.

LITTLEMUS

(*Worried*) Does that mean you <u>oppose</u> Caesar?

CICERO

Jupiter, no! Dumb old friend, I may be, but <u>stupid</u> — never. Oppose Caesar — no!

LITTLEMUS

Hum? I hope.

CICERO

This plan's <u>short run</u>, my life expectancy will exceed, I'm sure. The <u>long run</u>, only do my questions highlight.

LITTLEMUS

Logical, I guess.

CICERO

Hades, I expect to be with Jupiter in the long run. <u>Him</u>, I have a few questions for <u>too</u>. Definitely.

LITTLEMUS

Good. Caesar needs all the allies he can muster. But, I
<u>was</u> worried. I hoped not to have to report you.

CICERO

I play the game also, Littlemus. And well, so far.

POMPEIA

Come everyone. Come on. Gather round, Caesar's on
the Box.

TERENTIA

Must I? I rarely understand him. Always seems like he's
talking in code. Like to his soldiers, plotting some great
secret campaign.

POMPEIA

Right, dear. Have some food to occupy your mind.

TERENTIA

Wonderful idea.

CATALINA

Here we go again.

CATO

Hate these speeches. Not my cup of — what, what's —
that Persian stuff called, dear?

TERENTIA

Tea? Or do you mean opium?

CATO

Tea! I'll keep my brain, thank you.

TERENTIA

What's Caesar's line tonight, Pompeia?

POMPEIA

Don't know, never confides in me. Should be interesting.
Restless all day and didn't sleep at all.

CATO

(*Whispers to Catalina*) Probably with Servilia.

CATALINA

Your sister? His mistress?

CATO

Don't act surprised. All Rome knows. Good riddance is
all I say. Gods I hate him.

CATALINA

I didn't know.

CATO

What do you know?

CATALINA

I hate these kind of talks.

CATO

What kind?

CATALINA

Beating the drum kind. Always feel I miss something.

CATO

Oh, you mean the old war thing: "Protect our life style
and dribble." Or do you just hate war? (*Laughs*) As long
as not our — legs and arms.

CATALINA

Detached arms, legs, guts. I have no taste for, but small
price to pay for the rewards.

CATO

Beat the drum, then. You must agree with Littlemus, it
seems, and the need to arm the Gauls.

CATALINA

Well, not sold on that idea. War profits without war,
though, is a nice tune.

CATO

In Aphrodite's dreams!

CATALINA

Ya, silly. Our plan's better.

POMPEIA

(*Excited*) There he is!

TERENTIA

How's he get in that box? It's so small. And be
everywhere?

POMPEIA

(*Laughing*) He's an immortal, Terentia. Omnipotent.
Omnipresent. A God. All is possible.

TERENTIA

Oh, ya.

CATALINA

More wine. (*Yells to help*) More wine before he starts
again.

CICERO

Why do you peel all your grapes, Cato?

CATO

Poison. Seen it too often. Coat the skin with poison,

dries, don't see, taste or smell it then.

CICERO

I'll remember that next time I visit your house.

CATALINA

Heard he was to announce the freeing of all slaves
tonight.

CATO

In your dreams. Talk about gullible.

CICERO

I snatched up that tidbit too. I believe it's to increase the
tax base. If they work for pay, Caesar can tax it. Novel.

CATO

He'll do anything to get our money.

CATALINA

Taxes, taxes, taxes. And no sewers. Government!

LITTLEMUS

Take it to the Senate.

CATALINA

Why? They all bought their seats. Another of Caesar's
money makers. Stack the Senate with his people. All
bought and paid for to do his big business.

CATO

Dictator — never.

CICERO

Gods are funny like that.

CATALINA

Ha, ha. Anyway, they're all too rich in the Senate to
care about sewers. Just stay at their country houses. Let
us suffer.

CICERO

Clearly profits without war, — at work in that Senate
already.

CATO

Stuff it Cicero. Eat something. Occupy that tongue of
yours elsehow.

POMPEIA

Hush now, so can hear.

LITTLEMUS

(*Pulls Cicero aside*) Have you heard? Aurelia's money is
not enough for Catalina's debt. And he plots.

CICERO

Plots? I'll try him to the gallows for embezzlement.
Africa cries out.

LITTLEMUS

Caesar's a marked man in his eyes.

CICERO

Now, who should stop it! Catalina's no threat.

CATO

(*Comes over*) Littlemus you rat. A day with my troops
would cure you.

LITTLEMUS

Of what?

CATO

Wait and see.

LITTLEMUS

I hope, as they say, the plot does not thicken.

CATO

Oh, you little spy. (*Looks at Littlemus with malice*) My kingdom for good finances.

CICERO

You have no kingdom. Or finances for that matter.

CATO

The Ides are coming.

CICERO

The what?

CATO

He's on, come listen.

Hear J.C. on Box. Hear his voice in the background.

CAESAR

Friends, Romans, countrymen, lend me your ears again.

CATALINA

Needs a new speech writer.

CATO

Why? Nothing new to say.

Hear more mumbling from the Box but can't really make it out.

TERENTIA

What is this? Heard this before.

POMPEIA

But he makes it so exciting.

CAESAR

(*Voice from the Box*) To my loyal friends — a gift. The pots I sent earlier today with the do not open until later signs.

POMPEIA

Where?

CATO

(*Points to big earthen pot*) I guess that monstrosity.

TERENTIA

Open it.

CAESAR

(*From the Box*) <u>Don't</u> open the gift yet. I want all to happen on time. Wait for my command.

CATALINA

What's he up to?

CATO

Always wants to be in control. Thinks he's still a general.

CICERO

Littlemus, what gives?

LITTLEMUS

Wait —

CAESAR

(*Voice from the Box*) The time has come. Forget not to care for your family. Families are Rome's gift to the world. And foremost in your life.

CICERO

Littlemus, this sounds like a eulogy. What's up?

LITTLEMUS

Patience.

CAESAR

And, and honor the gods.

CATO

He's the God Prima Vera. By the Gods, he thinks he is.

CATALINA

I didn't expect this speech.

CATO

Whata you know? Nothing.

CICERO

Don't get it.

CAESAR

(*From box*) Remember — <u>family</u>!

POMPEIA

Antony, my gods, I forgot. You must get me home.
Before Caesar arrives. Come.

TERENTIA

Is that code? Care for the family.

POMPEIA

Shut up. Go.

LITTLEMUS

I forgot. I need to pick up a poultice for my wife. Cicero, accompany me.

CICERO

What? I need to hear the rest of the speech.

LITTLEMUS

Come, my good friend. Catalina, we must go. My wife is ill. I forgot, and must get her a poultice.

CATALINA

OK, but the speech.

LITTLEMUS

I'll read about it tomorrow. On the forum walls.

CATO

You're not leaving Pompeia? The speech has only started.

POMPEIA

But enough for me. Antony and I have other proffering.

CATALINA

Cicero, Terentia, Littlemus, Pompeia, Antony must you all go? The party's young. And we have so much food to eat.

CAESAR

(*Voice from the background*) Remember, family values is all. Family, family, family. And the Gods.

POMPEIA

(*Said quickly, in a hurry*) We must run.

CICERO

I can stay awhile.

LITTLEMUS

No, I need you.

POMPEIA

Yes, let's go.

TERENTIA

Still think that family stuff's code. The Gauls must be in real trouble.

LITTLEMUS

Come, let's <u>be off</u>. Quickly.

All dash out the door.

CAESAR

(*Voice from the background*) Open it (*Harsh commanding voice*). Open it <u>NOW!</u> Open the luxurious clay pots, now. My gift.

CATO

A gift from Caesar? Maybe he sees our way at last? There is hope for us.

CATALINA

I don't know. Doesn't he have Greek blood in him somewhere?

CATO

No! He needs us. Yes, Rome will survive now that we're reading from the same papyrus.

Catalina opens the pot. Loud noise and much smoke emanated from the pot. Lights on both sides of the stage come on showing

Patriarchs and servants dying.

CAESAR

(*As bodies fall in death throws, his voice comes over the Box*) This weapon, which will secure our new alliances, our security, our commerce, was developed in secret and kills within 5 minutes. But then the chosen ones already know that. Others, join me in this future world that I propose. Peace will reign. Rome blossoms again. Remember, you are either with me or against me — that is the ultimate Rome-Land security. — Sleep well.

CURTAIN FALLS

TWO I'S

Don Quiett

(Two Act Play)

To Cari

Acknowledgements

Perspective and perception philosophies were gleaned from the writings of Hyemeyohst Storm and Rumi. I thank them. Other writer's points, quoted in the play, are cited in the dialogue. And I thank them, too. Also, David Sirota, Norman Soloman, Mark Miller and Joe Conason must be thanked, as well, for their insights.

ACT I

SETTING:

Suburban living room/dining room with various work areas scattered around. For example, a mini painting area in one corner. A writing area in another. Many books.

CHARACTERS:

Bill – Struggling artist with new age thoughts.
Taylor – Writer. Quotes old writers and calls himself a writer, but rarely writes.
Eugene – Stockbroker, conservative, capitalist, confident of opinions.
Kris –Lawyer.
Dr. Ida – Veterinarian, idealist, confused.

CURTAIN RISES

Eugene has just come in the front door. Bill is in his 'studio' corner of the living room cleaning up his paint stuff. Kris is setting the table for dinner.

EUGENE
(*On entering room*) Hey, Bill. Kris. What's on the menu?

KRIS
Good to see you, Eugene. Indian. You know how Bill likes his hot curry.

EUGENE

(Said slowly) Great. Notice the sarcasm. Guess I don't eat. Maybe I should go over to Helen and Bob's.

BILL

Adventure, Eugene. Adventure some. Won't kill you. How's the market?

EUGENE

Usual. Like an elevator. Fortunately, I get on and off at the right floors.

BILL

So, you can buy a painting!

EUGENE

In your dreams. Waste is not in my portfolio.

KRIS

Don't worry, Eugene. We have a specially made wimpy curry just for you. Bill, come on, help me with the table.

BILL

Be right there.

EUGENE

(Whispers) Damn, Bill. You're so hen-pecked. Be assertive. Manly. Tell her it's not your job.

BILL

Grow up.

EUGENE

(As if didn't talk to Bill) Well, Kris, talking of portfolios, should we get together on yours? Lawyers are terrible market players and it is about time.

Ida runs into room through front door, slams door and ducks behind a window curtain. All talk is inhibited, stare towards Ida, then all talk over each other while Ida hides.

EUGENE

What the hell are you doing? (*Pauses*) Ida?

BILL

Hello. Earth to Ida.

IDA

(*From behind curtain*) Give you one guess.

EUGENE

Hiding?

IDA

Give the man a ci — guaa — r.

EUGENE

From what?

IDA

(*Fast,* angry) Won't get me. Didn't do nothin'. No matter what they say.

KRIS

Can I help?

IDA

(*Still behind curtain*) Ya. No. Who knows. War is peace. It's hell! More like it.

KRIS

Make sense. Try me. Remember, I'm your lawyer.

IDA

Malpractice, this is not.

KRIS

Come on, come out from behind there. Trust us. Test my lawyering.

IDA

Can't trust anyone.

EUGENE

Get out here Ida! Stop being a fool. No one has time for your neuroses. (*Pause*) Whaddaya think, Bill? A painting in this? Ida breeching the window womb.

BILL

U — gene! Ida, running from something? Hommie down boys?

KRIS

Bill, street smarts. You have none. Forget it.

IDA

(*Yells*) Po — Lee — ccce.

BILL

No, what? You're a vet. Cops don't chase veterinarians.

IDA

(*Yells*) Aaaahhh!

EUGENE

(*Laughing*) Skimming again?

KRIS

Really now, Ida. Remember — .

EUGENE
(*Breaks in*) — stocks are up. America's great —

KRIS
(*Shuts Eugene up with stare and talks over*) — remember reality? Remember?

IDA
Ha!

EUGENE
— it's a great day. Yes, great day, at least for a stock broker.

IDA
(*Angry, emotional*) <u>Fear</u>. Some reality. Horse kick in the head would be a more welcome fear.

KRIS
Ida, a little dramatic isn't it?

BILL
God, the passion. I <u>should</u> paint this! (*Jumps up and goes to easel*) Idaites!

EUGENE
No wonder you don't sell. Can't paint what can't see.

IDA
(*Said rapidly with anger*) Laugh if you want. But fearing suicide mall bombers, subway bombers, what-the-heck-bombers, identity theft, bank theft, Social Security collapse, crazy people, airport check in, road rage, home price bust, hurricanes, monsoon rains, debts, God-all the types of debts, school shooters, random shootings, the obesity epidemic, medical complications, food contamination, <u>are nothing</u> compared to this new fear.

<u>Nothing!</u>

All silent, then a knock at the door.

                          IDA
Oh, God. They're here!

                          KRIS

Who?

                          IDA

Them!

                          BILL
This is stupid. (*Goes to open door*) Ida, those fears are
90% political propaganda. Hi, Taylor. Dinner's not —

                          TAYLOR
Is that Ida in the window?

                          BILL
— not ready yet. Don't ask.

                          KRIS
Hey, Taylor. Little crisis here.

                          TAYLOR
Do I win something for finding Ida?

                          IDA
(*Yells*) Aaaahhh!

                          KRIS
Well, Ida — what is this? Car accidents - need to worry
about. Not this stuff. In U.S.

TAYLOR

Maybe I should —.

EUGENE

(*Breaks in*) — no you shouldn't. This could be good.

BILL

Ya, with a living, live audience, witnessing — <u>the break
down</u>.

TAYLOR

— should come back.

BILL

See it now, my <u>own</u> Munch "Scream" painting. And I
dedicate it to Ida. My muse.

IDA

(*Still behind curtain. Yells*) Aaaahhh!

BILL

Great!

KRIS

Ida, what <u>are</u> you afraid of?

IDA

Damn you pissants — <u>the government</u>!

EUGENE

(*Laughs*) They don't even know you exist.

KRIS

Ida, come out. Enlighten us.

IDA

You sure that's Taylor? Not some boot jack?

BILL

A what?

KRIS

Come on Ida.

TAYLOR

Swear it's me.

Ida peeks out, then emerges slowly.

EUGENE

Man, you're soakin' wet. Sweat? Hey, Bill: A sweaty
screamer. <u>Brilliant!</u>

Ida goes to mirror, wipes face, fixes hair.

KRIS

The fear, Ida, what could get you <u>this</u> worked up?

IDA

(*Still looking into mirror*) Black suited, sunglassesd guys
showing up at the veterinary clinic.

EUGENE

(*Laughs*) Sick pigs are good for business.

IDA

Ya, right. Me, I skedaddled out the back.

KRIS

Quit it, Eugene. Ida, why?

IDA

Didn't wanna wait for the punch line, joke.

BILL

Huh?

EUGENE

Ditto.

IDA

Sent me an E-mail, said "<u>suspected</u>", a key word I hear —
of being an unlawful battlefield combatant or unlawful
non-combatant – something, and wanted to talk to me.

BILL

So, talk.

IDA

Not after what I read. Declared all U.S. a battlefield.
<u>God!</u>

EUGENE

Always a bad sign. Reading.

TAYLOR

Really, I'll come back for dinner when reality checks in.

KRIS

Stop it, you guys. Well, Ida?

IDA

(*Still at mirror*) Paper said new law — Military
Commissions Act or something — said even if I'm only
<u>suspected</u> of being a legal non-combatant or something I'm
in big shit. And I'm not talking Budweiser here.

EUGENE

Budweiser —? Ooohh — Clydesdale doodoo.

                                    IDA

Further, my habeas corpuscles are gone, dead and I have no
monopoly card.

                                 EUGENE

Monopoly?

                                   BILL

Jail, stupid. Think.

                                   KRIS

Anyway, why the fear? Habeas corpus, it's a right.

                                  TAYLOR

You've stared at that mirror long enough, Ida. What gives?
Checking out your Buffalo?

                                    IDA

No. My hair.

                                  TAYLOR

Talk to us.

                                   BILL

(*Bill stands erect, straight, arm at side, sticks chest out.
Said in a low mysterious voice*) Better yet, check your
image out in my mirror.

                                    IDA

What mirror? What's your problem?

                                   BILL

Come on. Look!

                                  TAYLOR

(*Comes over, stares at Bill like looking in a mirror*) I see it.
Greed, desire reflects from Bill's surface.

EUGENE

Blank page to me. Bill is.

KRIS

He would be. Plus, should add envy, hatred to Eugene's view.

EUGENE

I hate no one, what about you Bill?

BILL

A polished heart. That's me, what I see.

EUGENE

Delusional.

IDA

Idiots! Aaaah! What mirror?? It's just flaky Bill, the ethereal painter. Words, words, words for abstract shit. No mirror. None of us are mirrors.

BILL

Ha!

EUGENE

Great retort. But don't really get it.

KRIS

Be nice. Bill's just searching for his soul.

BILL

Ya. But check my mirror anyway, Ida.

TAYLOR

I've got to go. Soul?

EUGENE

I'm blank. Thank the God's for stock markets. That's the Great Mirror of Life in the sky. This drivel has no market value.

TAYLOR

(*Walks over and starts preaching, slightly sarcastic*) Wait. The mist recedes. The soul emerges. To see the artist's soul, look at what the artist creates. If no soul in work, not only is the viewer cheated, but the artist as well. All stays unknown. Cruelty, and this, are the greatest sins.

IDA

Aaah! I'm scared and all you talk about is nonsense. What should I do? Come on; what, turn myself in?

TAYLOR

Nonsense? Buffalo mirrors?

BILL

Should be right up a vet's alley. Buffaloes.

IDA

Huh?

TAYLOR

Ya, you know. Old Indian ways, teachings —

Bill still standing erect.

EUGENE

Hold on Bill, let me check out this high-faluting mirror in you.

TAYLOR

Cheeky, Eugene. Don't care about Indian lore either, huh? Huh? Huh?

EUGENE

(*Stands in front of Bill and acts like looking in mirror*) Not it Taylor. Just an epiphany. Something. I see — yes — I see — the mirror says we encounter people without religion or people who reason poorly — (*Falls down*) Whoo — awesome. Two peoples. Our mission, if choose to take the mirror, is to set them onto the proper path again — wow!

TAYLOR

Finally read the Balzac I gave you. About time.

EUGENE

(*Points*) Not me, it's Bill's mirror.

BILL

Who? Wha'd he paint?

TAYLOR

Balzac? Give me strength, oh Great Mysterious One.

IDA

Idiots, I repeat. Where's my help? And what's this about Indians?

KRIS

Ya, with the problems Native Americans have had with the government, maybe they could have gained insight — whaddaya think?

EUGENE

On what? Eradication? Genocide? Face it, we're into To–Ma-To — To-May-To stuff. Victims of what some sheep call progress others call it equality. I say progress, you say equality. Must be other choices. Me — I say life's shit.

TAYLOR

Balzac again. The mirror speaks, I'm afraid. Better re-
evaluate yourself Eugene.

EUGENE

Hump!

IDA

Esoteric crap. What about these buffalo mirrors? If you're
not going to consider my crisis or help.

BILL

(*Looking down at his belly*) Me, I agree with Eugene's first
insight – a blank page.

KRIS

Just paint, Bill. Skip that psychology — art junk.

BILL

Junk! Junk! Jung is junk?

KRIS

Put it to bed, Bill.

BILL

(*Sits, stand, sits, etc as Jung questions him — in a German
accent. Standing as Jung and says in Swiss/German
dialect*) Vhy do you paint son? (*Sits as self*) Translate my
emotions into images. (*Standing as Jung*) Ahh, you vant
to find invard calm, reassurance. (*Sits as self*) Yes, to find
my inner self, original man.

KRIS

Stop it. Ida, —

BILL

(*Ignores Kris. Stands as Jung*) You mean to find religion.

You've lost it? (*Sits as self*) Whoo. Religion? (*Stands as Jung*) Vhat two question must religion answer?
(*Sits as self*) One, am I from a monkey? Two, what's with the platypus? (*Stands and yells as Jung*) No! Vhy do I exist? And am I insignificant unrelated or related to the surrounding universe and if so, how?

EUGENE
Excuse me, but isn't that three?

BILL
(*Sits as self*) So, that's the heart of any religion? (*Stand as Jung*). If vant to survive sanely in dis world we know. (*Sits as self*) Wow! Art, painting is religion. All should paint!

EUGENE
Guess, that's why they cut non-essential education art programs. Makes sense now. Separation of church and state stuff. Now I see.

KRIS
Can we get back to Ida?

TAYLOR
(*Standing up like lecturing*) George Sand said, if I recall correctly from my studies, something like — as far as I'm concerned organized religion is a mendacious cover-up — an insurmountable obstacle to the sacred. — she might agree painting should be the new religion for interpreting — (*Say slowly*) — the sublime Gospels.

IDA
This is really a lot of help. God! My ass is going to end up tortured somewhere in secret for something I didn't do. And I have to listen to this. Shit.

BILL

Now, you know why I see blank pages in my mirror. Pages to fill. <u>Jung's</u> cool, I like <u>his</u>, — "painting is the universal religion."

EUGENE

Maybe I'm wrong, being only a practical stockbroker, but Bill you were both — Jung was absent.

BILL

That's why you're 'F—ed' up. A blank page flapping in the wind. Drugs are a false God. Money is not everything.

EUGENE

Me, drugs? My feet are firmly planted on this Earth. My blank pages are just blank, not flapping, drug blank.

KRIS

Yes, let's get back to earth. Ida, what is it?

TAYLOR

My writer's mind says, "You will shape your world only by changing what exists within you." An oollldd Indian proverb.

BILL

Ya, ghettos don't shape people. People shape ghettos.

KRIS

What the hell?

IDA

Buffalo mirrors? Buffalo mirrors? Hell. Where's the beef?

BILL

Ok, ok, let's help Ida. <u>For real</u>. Even if it seems anticlimactic at this point. Well, here goes, Indians basically were taught to see mirrors in all things. Called buffalo mirrors, since the buffalo was all things to them for life. Therefore, what you saw in these mirrors was a reflection of you. <u>You</u> are in all things. If you didn't like what saw, change it within you. You and God are in all things. That's as brief a bird's eye view of buffalo mirrors as I can manage.

TAYLOR

That sounds Christiany.

BILL

Yep, a universality.

IDA

Shit. — Aaaah! What help is that?

KRIS

What, Ida, what <u>is</u> your problem? Can't help till we know.

TAYLOR

Wait a minute. This reminds me of the Greeks or Sufis or somebody.

EUGENE

Greeks! Gifts? We better keep an eye on T.

IDA

Idiots. Guess we do have the government we deserve.

KRIS

Ida, what is it?

TAYLOR

No, listen. Had to do with who were the best painters in the world. Chinese or Greeks.

BILL

(*Excited*) Dynamite, I remember that.

IDA

(*Shouts. Then just sits, squirms, slumps, hides as talks*)
<u>Reality</u>? Remember it? Could we get back to it? <u>Help me</u>!

EUGENE

(*Ignores Ida*) Seems to me —

IDA

Who cares?!

EUGENE

— it would appear we have many cracked mirrors here.

IDA

Here? I think you can expand that. To all man. Fuckin'
government.

EUGENE

I didn't know you were a Republican. Anti-government.

Ida slumps, collapses into a chair.

TAYLOR

(*Oblivious to conversation*) Anyway, the king Sufi or
someone challenged them to see who the best painters
were. Chinese demanded all the paints available.

BILL

(*Excited*) Ya, right. I recall. And the dumb Greeks asked
for polish.

TAYLOR

(*Like telling a secret, a story*) They where then isolated in
adjoining rooms. After a time, the king showed up to

judge. First, he checks the Chinese room. The colors and paintings were brilliant. Beautiful.

BILL

(*Jumps up, dashes to his easel and turns easel around for all to see his work*) — da, daa.

EUGENE

Dreaming again, Bill? Brilliant eludes your work.

TAYLOR

Then the king slides the curtain back exposing the Greek side. The super duper polished surfaces reflected the Chinese paintings. All were bedazzled. The paintings were more beautiful than before.

KRIS

Is there a point to this? Or do I plead to the judge for irrelevancy? Ida waits.

BILL

Dualism, inner – outer self!

KRIS

Oh, shit. Why can't painters just paint. Pretty stuff. Know what I mean?

TAYLOR

Personally, believe Bill's dilemma has something to do with passing beyond the outer form of things.

KRIS

What the helllll —

BILL

(*Yells excitedly*) "Pure heart" equals the polished mirror! Get it?

EUGENE

Need more practice then — old Bill.

BILL

Polish, light, light in all things, Christianity. Get it?

EUGENE

No. My advice Bill — practice makes perfect.

BILL

Go to hell, my good buddy. Ha, ha.

TAYLOR

For me, the writer, it says to be chained by my own beliefs
is bad enough, heaven knows; but to be chained by other
people's is monstrous. To quote the great mystery writer
— Anne Perry. Cracked mirrors or polished ones —
irrelevant.

IDA

(*Exhausted*) I don't understand?

BILL

Geesh, saying nobody has the right to decide what other
people want or feel.

TAYLOR

(*Like on soap box*) Physical image on paper – elevated to
the spiritual — is the freedom you seek. Right Bill?

BILL

Polished mirrors — ultimate dualism. Ya!!

IDA

I still don't understand.

BILL

Try this then. The real me. My essence is inside and is
not what you see. Like — get into a car, but are not the
car. See now? Jesus stuff.

IDA

I need a drink. Baileys, please.

EUGENE

Let me get this right: The earth's just one big parking lot
and your body is a car occupying one of the said spaces?

BILL

Correctomundo!

EUGENE

And — let me be clear, precise, accurate, definitive or
whatever. After all, I'm only a concrete Wall Street kinda
guy. And <u>that</u> is why you paint?

BILL

You got it!

EUGENE

Christ! What do I got? A moronic friend? Think this will
help you sell? Personally, doubt it.

TAYLOR

See the point though.

BILL

God, another one.

TAYLOR

No, listen.

EUGENE
Sex! You guys need sex. Might help, think it over.

TAYLOR
Everything's not answered with sex.

EUGENE
Kidding, right?

TAYLOR
You're missing the point, Eugene. Quoting Picasso, "Psychotherapy's nice, but we have to paint it."

EUGENE
Psychobabble! Bull! Guess, though, it is the only way to explain that shit of yours. (*Throws paint on canvas*)

BILL
Sound like my mother. (*Uses high old lady voice*) "Why don't you paint barns, old shoes, portraits? They sell! Plus you do them so well. Don't know what the rest of this crap is."

EUGENE
She's right.

BILL
She never understood my crack in the world series. Cosmic eggs.

EUGENE
(*Laughing*) I thought it was cracked too.

TAYLOR
Cosmic egg — cosmic art — way above your pay grade, Eugene. That's for sure.

EUGENE

Ready for supper, Taylor. Got a nice knuckle sandwich just waiting for you.

TAYLOR

Will you ever outgrow that play ground crap?

EUGENE

No. World needs an inquisition.

TAYLOR

You mean, inquisitor?

EUGENE

No. Smart-ass. I'm the whole damn thing.

KRIS

(*Bangs head on wall*) Que pasa? Que pasa?

EUGENE

Bill thinks he's a car.

KRIS

Como?

TAYLOR

Spanish lessons again, huh?

KRIS

(*Exasperated*) Ya, but it's not taking. The country's passing me by. What about the car?

BILL

Well, when one gets into a car, you don't become the car. Right? Well, we get into these bodies and we're not the bodies.

TAYLOR

Thus, the earth is an overcrowded, becoming more so, parking lot.

EUGENE

Stuff it, you guys.

KRIS

The point Bill. You're a dinosaur? Or non-existent? What?

BILL

Don't know. That's why I paint — da-da-da-daaa. To find the "Original Man" within.

EUGENE

The driver? Christ, you're weirder by the minute. Any games on T.V. tonight? Love hockey.

TAYLOR

(*Stands up, recites*) Painting is a companion with whom one may hope to walk a great part of life's journey. Age cannot wither her, nor custom stale her infinite variety.

BILL

That was great! Who said that? Blake? Keats? Da Vinci? Odelon Redon?

TAYLOR

Churchill of the Winston variety. Another painter!

BILL

Well, I agree with him, all people should paint.

KRIS

Whose Oddie — Od — whatever? Are we back to your "Difficult Art" definition again?

BILL

Yes, the pressure is there for all.

EUGENE

To paint? Does bull hockey ring a bell?

BILL

(*Said sympathetically, and with understanding*) The search internally for an understanding and enlightenment can only be gained thusly. Paint. Life's demand. Religion.

EUGENE

Hockey. That's life's demand. Gives you the same stuff. You artsy <u>fartsy</u> people are all alike.

TAYLOR

He was not referring to innards and puke. His ethereal search was loftier.

EUGENE

Kiss my ascot, Taylor.

KRIS

To change subjects, how's the book coming, Taylor?

IDA

Ooooh. What about me?

EUGENE

Book's not as good as my stocks, Kris. (*Laughs*) I bet.

BILL

You need to sculpt again, Eugene. Relaxes you. But talk about weird. Yet, metal trinkets that tickled the little grey cells, you definitely do produce.

EUGENE

Sculpting sucks. Prefer the gigantic profits of stock gambling.

IDA

(*Looks out window. More antsy*) Assholes. You guys are assholes worrying about that stuff. Please. Help me. They're after me.

KRIS

Que?

IDA

(*Whines*) Come on, Kris.

KRIS

Ok.

EUGENE

Wait a minute. If I'm not paranoid, you people are suggesting money's not all? Everything?! Piss off. Jesus owned his own robe. End of story.

KRIS

Como?

EUGENE

Pope knows. That's why the church has so much money. Robe justified it.

All look at Eugene.

EUGENE

It did! You know, riches are OK. Personal wealth.

IDA

Kr —

KRIS

In a minute Ida. So, if <u>He</u> rented his robe <u>and</u> maybe married or killed less people — oh wait, he didn't kill people —

EUGENE

Get off the rag, Kris.

KRIS

Well, if rented and married maybe would have less problems in the world. Is that your point?

EUGENE

Could be. Remember, greed is good, as they say. You guys just can't handle it. Weaklings. Hide behind words.

BILL

Me — thinks you see too many movies.

KRIS

I declare Don Quixote's dead.

EUGENE

(*Laughs*) Brain washed. Ring a bell? You guys could be replaced by an empty space and be far more effective.

IDA

(*Pleading*) Can we get to my problem?

KRIS

Right, what is it?

IDA

Thank you. Remember that International Veterinary meeting I went to in Sa — oww — di Arabia?

KRIS

Ya.

BILL

(*Laughing*) Who could forget your weeks of pre-flight panic?

EUGENE

Phobia. An inadequate word. Definitely.

KRIS

Go on.

IDA

Well, I was on a panel looking at preventing Foreign Animal Diseases. Disease not in our country, eradicated here years ago. And why our animals produce so well.

TAYLOR

Cute verbiage. Foreign to who?

IDA

Right. Foreign to us. To them it's endemic.

EUGENE

Know I'm slow, but this has great potential for terrorism. Doesn't it? Hell could —

IDA

(*Breaks in*) Bingo! That's why I'm a "person of interest."

TAYLOR

Verbiage again.

BILL

This is nothing. Let's talk more painting — religion.

IDA

I wish! Anyway sent email to a delegate from Iran, nice young vet, about airport's lack of scrutiny on my return. Checked nothing, disinfected nothing. Supposed to.

TAYLOR

Doubt go to jail for that.

IDA

Probably not, but added how easy it would be to sneak foot-and-mouth disease virus and the like into the States on returning from "endemic" countries like in Africa, Asia, South America. Chuckled about how easy it would be to get a small vial in, which could decimate our cattle production. We correspond regularly, professionally, now.

KRIS

Primo stupid. NSA bait. I hope you didn't call.

IDA

Well —

KRIS

No wonder you're a <u>suspected</u> terrorist, legal combatant.

BILL

Could always paint. Become religious.

EUGENE

Get off religion. Painting is <u>no religion</u>.

TAYLOR

Wait a minute Eugene, Bill could have something here.

EUGENE

Geesh. You artsy people are all alike. No reality. Nothing but Idealists. Losers.

BILL

Idealists — a stockbroker's dirty four letter word.

TAYLOR

Tolstoy, if I remember said something like, "— there will always be a private and secret revolution in man from which a new religion will be born — no name — but will be comforting making life possible."

BILL

Hey, man. I'm in good company. Me — Tolstoy.

EUGENE

Ida's right. Asshole you are. Money's the revolution.

IDA

Damn, do you even care about me? My plight?

KRIS

Sure, but think you're over reacting.

IDA

Like hell! Those sunglasses were real.

BILL

(*Goes to easel area*) Come on, Ida. Paint. Be born again. Better than hiding.

IDA

(*Yells*) Aaagh! Can't paint. Not even a straight line.

BILL

Ha! Kandinsky said, "if paint with the soul's eye, can't do it wrong." You can paint Ida. Really. All can.

EUGENE

Are we back in that car? With a soulful drive?

IDA

(*Earnestly*) Please guys, I'm scared. How could any congressman vote for that Military Commissions Act?

BILL

Blindly.

EUGENE

We're at WAR folks. Don't you know?

TAYLOR

Ya, seems <u>rights</u> go out the window <u>in War.</u>

BILL

Should be opposite — somehow. Think about it.

All are quiet for a minute, look at each other.

EUGENE

(*Bursts out*) War's War. Unitarian Executive rules.

IDA

(*Shakes head. Pleading*) What do I do?

BILL

To me, it all boils down to — we are not taught to experience something, but to intellectualize it, which gives the <u>illusion</u> of an understanding, experience.

EUGENE

Where do you get this crap, Bill? You need a life. Less time being by yourself.

IDA

I don't even know what he means. How's it help?

                          TAYLOR
Well, speaking of my favorite detective —

                          EUGENE
Who? Not me.

                          BILL
<u>What did</u> she paint?

                          TAYLOR
— said, "greatest power sometime lies in not doing a
thing."

                          IDA
Just keep hiding?

                          TAYLOR
(*Acts out detective like*) — It's so easy to use a skill simply
because you have it, and not look two — three steps ahead
to see what it may cause."

                          IDA
Plead guilty? Turn myself in? I'm <u>no</u> terrorist.

                          EUGENE
Eat more apple pies. Wave flags a lot. Flood your car with
patriotic bumper stickers. Prove patriotism.

                          KRIS
No. No. Get serious here for a minute. This new Act
could be problematic.

                          BILL
Well, Ida, if you suddenly disappear, we'll beat the bushes
stirring up a stink until we find you. Secrets not
withstanding. Or habeas corpus for that matter.

TAYLOR

Think that's a mixed metaphor.

BILL

But appropriate.

IDA

Aaaah!

TAYLOR

A thought, if secret trials win, follow Balzac's advice ala Swedenborg: between God and man there exists a physical world populated by angels who live as we do —

IDA

Shit!

TAYLOR

— rise above the misery of fellow prisoners to attend to their salvation, be a new angel.

IDA

Go to (*Spell out*) H-E- L- L.

TAYLOR

(*Chuckles*) Trying singularly to interject some humor here, get us back to the real world. Not the world of government or fear.

BILL

Real world. That's it! Let's try an experiment.

KRIS

Not now, Bill.

EUGENE

Couldn't hurt. Well, maybe — it could.

KRIS

Let me call my law firm. Get more senior advice.

BILL

No wait. Me first.

EUGENE

Kris, watch what you say. May be bugged.

TAYLOR

(*Said conspiratorially*) The paranoia — fear — suspicion grows. All that's missing is the Enabling Act!

BILL

Wait now. Come on. Get in a circle. I'm going to turn the lights out, bring something in. You guys touch it from <u>where you're standing</u> and tell me what it really is. Wait now. No cheating.

All lights go out, hear scraping, all mumble. People complain, say "this is stupid" etc. in dark waiting.

BILL

OK, reach out and say what feel.

IDA

Oh God! <u>Where art thou</u>?

EUGENE

From where I stand it's a bunch of tall round pipes spreading out, fan like.

KRIS

No, it's low and flat.

TAYLOR

Short, 2 by 2, with four balls, like ears, in corners.

IDA

Did I mention stupid, dumb. I feel nothing.

EUGENE

Wait, if I kneel now I feel short square pipes.

BILL

Well, what is it?

All speak together like — Eugene yells out — antique high backed wicker chair; Kris — hallway, low narrow table, Ida — nothing, Taylor — Chinese flower pot.

BILL

Ok, let me get the lights.

Lights come on and see a Bowflex type workout machine with all people in their position touching different parts.

IDA

You're nuts Bill. An exercise machine! How the hell is this going to help?

BILL

Get you back to reality. Trample your fear.

IDA

The law <u>is a real fear</u>! I'm cooked.

KRIS

Well, we do still have free speech.

BILL

There you go.

KRIS

If we get you to our offices, could act as a sanctuary, so

can't snatch you away to the void.

                              IDA
I wouldn't make a good angel.

                              BILL
See what reality does?

All stop and stare at Bill

                              BILL
What?

                              TAYLOR
That dark stunt's an old Sufi — oh — oh — whatever,
isn't it?

                              BILL
Ya, but I couldn't get an elephant.

                              EUGENE
Elephant? Ugh. So, what we did was use a bodily sense,
reach a wrong conclusion — because — of our particular
standpoint?

                              BILL
Don't know why they say you're so dumb.

                              EUGENE
Eeerrrh!

                              TAYLOR
If I recall, believe it illustrates our human limitations.
Something like ocean of reality and we only get hit with
the spray. Basically don't see the big picture.

BILL

(*Excited*) Right. State of separation. Dualism. I'm not the car, stupid.

EUGENE

Car's again! Basically, we don't know shit. And never will.

BILL

Showing your blank page again. Wind flapping.

TAYLOR

Wake up Eugene. Means: must empower your senses. Develop true self. Reality may not be reality.

BILL

Yes, find your Original Man within. Soul's eye! Paint!

IDA

(*Depressed and shakes head*) Shit. See <u>my</u> future right before my eyes.

BILL

Great!!

IDA

(*Walks around, shakes head*) The ocean of reality's foam — Military Commission Act — hits me between the eyes and I overcome my limitations to soar angelically with Swedenborg's angels elevating my fellow cell mates by blowing more Ocean foam into their eyes. Some plan — or I paint.

TAYLOR

Not sure that's the Sufi Way, to quote someone.

KRIS

I better make that call.

TAYLOR

Wait a minute, this is kinda like that Indian stuff.

BILL

What stuff?

TAYLOR

You know, their teaching.

BILL

Teaching?

TAYLOR

Damn, don't you remember anything long-term Bill?

EUGENE

(*Sings*) 'Dream along with me'. Bill — remember.
Oxymoron.

TAYLOR

You even tried to paint it, remember? Chief sits warriors in
a circle and puts an object in the middle, like a feather.
Then asked them to describe it. Some said long flat, others
a circle etc. depending on point of view in the circle.
Chief then asked who was correct. Answer — all.
Depends on perspective. Things may not be as seem.
Buffalo mirrors.

BILL

Oh, ya! Ya! My circle phase. Loved it.

IDA

You're sick, Bill. Sick. Be less painful to your friends if just
cut your ear off.

BILL

Do you think?

IDA

Aaaagh!

EUGENE

Flaky. Hum, hum. Humph. (*Becomes very serious*) Let's try a business point of view regarding this dilemma. Huh? For a little <u>real</u> reality.

IDA

Forget it. I'll just jump out the window. Too much foam manure for this angel.

Bill slides machine off stage as others talk.

EUGENE

Take Taylor —

IDA

Ha! You take him.

EUGENE

Uumph. Anyway, he wants to publish. Print a book for the commercial market, expects financial rewards. <u>That's business</u>. If you wish to vanquish indigence, must get them to do it themselves.

TAYLOR

Your Balzac interpretations seem dangerous.

IDA

Christ. Eugene, you have no idea what's going on. Do you? What we're talking about.

EUGENE

Sure I do. Government is business. Your problem is <u>not</u>
good business. Thus, no problem. You're no indigent,
therefore no problem. Good business.

IDA

U-uuuu-ow. (*Yells*) They're trying to declare me a
terrorist.

EUGENE

Right. My point exactly. Bad business for Americans.

KRIS

(*Exasperated*) Wonder if the German populace felt that
way in the 30's.

EUGENE

(*Angry*) Come off it. If you can change thought, you can
change the world. Good business.

KRIS

Think you just made my point.

EUGENE

Listen Ida, all you need to do is redefine yourself.

IDA

Whaaaat? From what – a terrorist?

KRIS

Wouldn't that be re-redefine then? Vet — terrorist —
nuclear physicist.

IDA

Holy shit. I don't know who's more daft, you guys or the
government.

EUGENE

No. Just good business sense. Unless —yes, unless you can afford a lobbyist.

IDA

Come again. Redefine myself or hire a lobbyist?

TAYLOR

(*Laughing during run-on sentence*) Ha, ha! Eugene's answer to everything. Thinks it's natural. Fair. Ok. Like one day a lobbyist, next in government, then lobbyist again, then government, lobbyist, government, etc, etc, etc. So, get stuff like top drug company lobbyist becoming top government Department of Health designee who gives birth to a Medicare Bill resulting in billions for drug company. Good business.

IDA

(*Questioningly*) Saying I need an ex-Justice Department person - masquerading as a lawyer — who in reality is a lobbyist with a business interest — that my potential case may aid and abet for business growth?

EUGENE

That's the game. Business rules. Real reality. Lobbyists.

IDA

(*Pleads*) Kris? (*Silence*) Well?

KRIS

I better call the office. (*Goes to phone and calls*)

TAYLOR

Eugene's a cynic. This has to be just a huge misunderstanding.

IDA

Worse than a dream, I can tell you. Because, I <u>can't</u> wake up.

KRIS

(*At phone*) Ah huh. Hum. OK. Ya. Really. (*Hangs up and sits down*) Talk about Clydesdales. Where do I start?

EUGENE

(*Jumps in*) Or, I hate to use this analogy or whatever, you could take a page out of Hitler's playbook.

IDA

Lord give me strength. Hitler?

EUGENE

Not the bad parts, but the "Big Lie!" So, better get to the press. <u>And quick</u>!

IDA

(*Slaps her face and looks around slowly*) Nope. Still here. Hoped I was in dreamland and this would <u>all</u> be vanquished.

TAYLOR

Your point Eugene? I can't wait.

KRIS

We may only be digging the hole deeper. Think about it. The advice I —.

EUGENE

(*Breaks in*) It could work. Hear me out.

IDA

Or, to be shot for treason. (*Pause*) I'll listen.

EUGENE

First is the "talking point." A trick the executive branch uses regularly. Make a <u>wholly false</u> assertion, repeat it often. Be an assured liar. Authoritative liar. Convincing. But lie, lie, lie with absolute assurance it's the truth.

IDA

The truth's not good enough? <u>I did nothing</u>!

TAYLOR

Sound like a mob boss. (*Dialect*) I did nothin'.

EUGENE

Right. Lies are the best truth.

KRIS

Do you think Presidents, Hitler even, knew they were lying?

EUGENE

Probably, at one time. Now, doubt if can remember.

IDA

Kidding again. Right?

TAYLOR

Revisionist history has <u>touched down</u>. Like when said Sad — damn threw inspectors out of Iraq, when in reality <u>we</u> told them to leave.

EUGENE

Da daaa. The plot thickens. The next step evokes the big 'G.O.' — George Orwell. And his 'double think'. Ask President Jr.

TAYLOR

You should be the writer. Your imagination is wasted on

stocks. Far better than mine.

                    EUGENE
Funny. Ha, ha. I'm just a realist.

                     IDA
With your logic, guess I need to besmirch the FBI or NSA
or whoever is after me.

                    EUGENE
God, you're quick.

                     IDA
Get out.

                    EUGENE
Works for Presidents. Accuse your enemy of committing
the crime you plan. The 'disorienting tactic.'

                     KRIS
How about you becoming a lawyer? Huh, Eugene?

                    EUGENE
I'm all things. Good businessmen are. Anyway, remember
when Bush accused Gore of out spending him and stealing
the election? Or remember his cocky flyboy attitude
declaring 'Mission Accomplished?' The big disorientating
tactic. Or the war on drugs — no one remembers that.
Commit to what they want, but have no plans to do it. I
rest my case. Obfuscate, disorientate interweave facts and
fiction. <u>Then</u> freedom awaits.

                     IDA
Boy, <u>does</u> this help. OK, I know no lobbyists, so that's out.
Therefore, I must <u>redefine</u> myself as innocent, since
authorities believe me a terrorist. <u>And</u> lie <u>big</u> and <u>boldly</u>
about my innocence. All these lies in the face of the facts.

(*Screams*) <u>Yet, I'm innocent</u>. Also, get my friends to lie, even though the lie's true.

TAYLOR
Holy Orwell, I'm getting confused.

EUGENE
Good.

IDA
(*Gets more agitated as speaks*) Good? Forget it. Then, I need to impugn those attacking me as being the true terrorists, jack-booted renegades. As authorities off the reservation covering up their own deeds.

EUGENE
Great. You could become a lobbyist.

IDA
I perpetuate the 'Big lie' with 'talking points' and 'disorientating tactics' ala double think to become something I'm not, <u>but really am</u>. <u>Has</u> to be a better way.

KRIS
Maybe we better talk Ida.

IDA
Please.

EUGENE
Or —

IDA
Euu-geee-ne. No offense, but I've heard enough from you. Some reality you see. But, thank you.

EUGENE

Liberals. Yuck.

KRIS

Eugene, stop it. Remember the elephant, feather.
Anyway, Ida, you have problems.

IDA

Tell me about it.

KRIS

While I waited for my senior partner's advice, they made
some calls. Calls way beyond my connections.

IDA

Great. Some action?

KRIS

Humm. Not really. Seems this <u>nice</u> guy of yours is a
known terrorist.

IDA

Get out. I saw pictures of his wife, kids, farm. He's just a
normal bloke. A veterinarian.

KRIS

Well, seems he works for a charity —

IDA

(*Jumps in*)I know. Distributes animals for backyard farms
so people become somewhat self sufficient and
independent. Rabbits, chickens, lambs. Teach how to
care for - animal husbandry. Quite successful. Positive
data he presented.

KRIS

The charity has links with terrorist groups.

IDA

Christ. That means nothing. Often only way to help poor in those areas. Join the system to beat it. Take Palestine.

KRIS

Not the point.

IDA

IRA's no different. Did good and bad. Good for now is winning. It can happen.

KRIS

Did you donate money?

IDA

Ya, $100 bucks.

KRIS

Well, there you see.

IDA

See what? Feed a family for a year. Shoot me!

KRIS

Might. You admit you have actively supported a terrorist organization, aided and abetted the enemy, and maintained communication abroad and at home with persons of interest from these groups.

IDA

(*Angry*) Holy fuck. It <u>was</u> a veterinary meeting. We shared how to best feed the poor shits of the world. And yes, we've stayed in touch to improve and increase those efforts.

KRIS

Well —

IDA

Well what? I thought I was being a good Christian,
American, Earthling, humanitarian.

KRIS

Battlefield combatant is how some see it. Eugene's lie
campaign may be the way.

TAYLOR

I thought the Tao was the way. Or Dancing Wu Li Master.

KRIS

Not a time for humor, Taylor.

IDA

Is it ever anymore? Come on guys, get real.

KRIS

My boss suggests with what the authorities have on you,
and it appears to be much, if you don't want to get to Git-
mo, get to Canada!

IDA

(*Yells*) Canada!

CURTAIN FALLS

ACT II

CURTAIN RISES

*Ida slumped on couch, being comforted by Kris. Others, except
Bill, in quiet general talk or wondering about Ida's plight.
Bill bursts into the room dressed in the battle armor of a
shining knight, like Halloween costume, of King Arthur's time.*

BILL

(*Swings sword to and fro attacking invisible enemies and
at last points at Eugene. Sings fight scene music from
Seahawks (Errol Flynn* movie*)* Da, da, daaa, da, da, daa.
The Wasteland must end!

EUGENE

You're nuts. When do we eat? Stay a painter Bill, you've
no future in acting.

BILL

(*Sword still at Eugene's throat*) No. King Arthur's
wasteland must be purged.

KRIS

Bill we have a serious problem here. Ida —

BILL

(*Points at others*) And King Arthur doesn't? Da-da-daa-
daaa.

TAYLOR

The King's dead.

BILL

(*Sword in air*) Long live the King!

EUGENE
Christ Bill. Get real. Didn't you hear anything I said.

BILL
Who couldn't hear that dribble? What was King Arthur's wasteland?

EUGENE
Dribble?!

TAYLOR
The assholes of that time period fought till England was burnt, scorched, from border to border. Irrelevant.

BILL
No. No. Symbol, like the entire Arthur Myth. Historical or not. It was land emanating not from life, but from controlling <u>powers</u>.

KRIS
(*Sarcastic*) Whoopee.

TAYLOR
Right, right. I get it. All is known. Ya. No quests to transverse. Only cliché to memorize or live out. Brilliant!

BILL
Hope. Da-da-dada-daaa. (*Hums Seahawk music*) I see hope in you Taylor. A land where creative personalities are blind.

EUGENE
Saying we live in one of these blind spots now? Humph. You better watch out for squirrels, is all I can say.

BILL
What a Dick head.

IDA

(*Sounding high strung*) Could be you're right there Bill.
The kitchen 'Table of the Round' definitely's called for.
How else can you explain U.S. preemptive striking?

KRIS

Ida? Relax.

TAYLOR

Take your painting. Well, not yours, but saleable art.
How else could you account for the mental illness of
paying $82 million, or even more, for a picture. Insane.

EUGENE

Ever hear of investments? Speculation?

BILL

The point, Eugene, is that a painting's more than money.

EUGENE

(*Laughs*) Ya, right. Reality check time folks. Come on.
It's no more than a stock prospectus.

TAYLOR

The more you talk Eugene, the more the wasteland
expands. Big time.

BILL

(*Sword in air*) To the kitchen round to plan, plot, our
strategy.

EUGENE

You mean to eat. I hope. Don't you?

BILL

No! No. To stimulate personal quests by the multitudes in
order to elevate the consciousness of all humankind.

TAYLOR

Me, I'm waiting for Godot.

EUGENE

Me, supper.

IDA

Me, jail.

KRIS

What do you think of Canada?

BILL

Cold.

IDA

(*Depressed*) Mental illness, mental illness. You're right,
Taylor. What, close to a trillion a year spent on the U.S.
military now? Prevention? Self defense my eye. Still
40,000 nukes. What the hell would they do blown up?
Billions for a missile defense screen and, yet, no one today
has missiles to hit us. Mental illness. Yep, now that's
mental illness. It's not just me.

EUGENE

<u>Business</u>! Good business. That's all you're talking about,
Ida. The mental ill ideas you possess would bankrupt the
country. Let's eat.

TAYLOR

I agree. <u>Time</u>, the boomeranging circle, where all stands
still. Man advances nowhere.

KRIS

Huh?

TAYLOR

Face it. Our species can't possibly match dinosaurs.

EUGENE

Que?

TAYLOR

OK. How long did they trod this earth?

BILL

Brilliant. Brilliant!

KRIS

Shit. Let's just help Ida.

EUGENE

Double Ida's Clydesdale business.

TAYLOR

The man species will never attain the age of a million, let alone the 168 million of our predecessors with our present sensitivities.

EUGENE

Pipe dreams are the true mental illness today.

TAYLOR

I rest my case. Extinction sniffs out it's new prey. Da-da, apparently we are it.

EUGENE

That extinction attitude is unproductive, especially when playing markets.

BILL

Playing? Markets? Extinction? The message clears, me thinks.

EUGENE

(*Angry. Speaks like talking to troops or pre-game tirade*)
Wastelands are not new. So piss off. We <u>shall</u> overcome!

BILL

Da-da-dada-dada-daaa. (*Sea Hawk's theme*) Eugene joins
the team! The fight! To vanquish the spiritual desert
spawned by concrete doctrines. Doctrines imposed by
education, politics and even religion this fine day.

EUGENE

Damn you. No way.

TAYLOR

Better than being a flapping in the wind blank page.

EUGENE

Wanna bet?

IDA

(*Breaking in, sounding hopeless*) Before I'm banished to
the wasteland of the wasteland, what's the game plan?

KRIS

Patience Ida. The law was not written with the <u>intent</u>, to
mean, how it's being used against you.

IDA

Why write such a <u>law</u> then?

TAYLOR

A better wasteland enabler, written as such.

BILL

Back to the issue —

EUGENE

Issue. No issue. Psychedelic college speak - is all.

TAYLOR

Double think?

EUGENE

Whatever.

TAYLOR

Time stops. No rolling wheel, only moss.

BILL

The issue, as I say, no <u>personal experience</u>, thus the wasteland and —

KRIS

(*Cuts in*) Beg to differ. Ida has more experience than can stand right now.

IDA

(*Exaspirated*) God, ought it to be this complicated. I was only warning of potential food animal production disasters, not planning attacks. Christ, I'm an American.

BILL

(*Excited, kid-like said fast*) Paint! All should partake of the "Ritual of Painting." In such, the original man within, soul, inner necessity can be <u>experienced</u> in a personal direct way, thus the wasteland will bloom with flowers. War — a failed myth.

EUGENE

Crap. That's why you have brown eyes. You're full of it. You must be smelling your paints, turpentine <u>way</u> too much. What non-sense. Flower child. Ha! I repeat, crap.

TAYLOR

Ah, the eternal stillness of time.

IDA

(*Goes to paint area, searches*) Pass me the turpentine. I need a good sniff. Only way it seems for me to cope with the lies hurled my way. Beyond lies, reason, on the fringe of pathology. KGB paranoia. Machiavellian.

TAYLOR

Does seem our goal is to match the evil of our enemy.

KRIS

What's their evidence Ida?

IDA

E-mails, phone conversations, travel to the Middle East. All circumstantial, and taken out of context very damning. (*Pauses*) Canada's looking better.

TAYLOR

We're not at war with Canada yet, are we?

EUGENE

Naw. Soon will be 'us' anyway, when the President's North American Union thing is stealthily treaty-ized.

KRIS

Congress will never allow it. Especially weakening our Constitution, as it does, and superceding our Bill of Rights.

EUGENE

Watch! Being off the radar, it's too late for them already. Plus, it's great for business.

IDA

Hallo, hello. Help! Aaagh!

KRIS

Hum. Canada maybe out.

TAYLOR

To quote a Sufi poet, "<u>Where's my ass?</u>"!

IDA

(*Sarcastically*) Aagh. Help at last — give-me- a-break.

TAYLOR

(*Laughing*) No. No. That's the punch line.

BILL

(*Optimistically*) Oh, ya! Ya. Doesn't it start like, "What's more significant, the words or what they transmit?"

TAYLOR

Bill's hot today. Basically —

IDA

Please, guys!

TAYLOR

— when you discard the shell and discover the kernel, you have entered the realm of <u>Jesus</u>. And, you will no longer say — that punch line.

IDA

(*Questioningly*) Where's my ass?

EUGENE

(*Also questioningly*) Sufi? Islam? What do <u>they</u> know about Jesus?

TAYLOR

Eugene, read <u>a</u> book. One preferably without stock quotes.

BILL

That's why all <u>must paint</u>! Kernel searching. Jesus
seeking.

IDA

Where ? New Zealand? Kris? Help me!

KRIS

After that, who knows where your ass should be.

TAYLOR

(*Picks up book from shelf to read*) The poem ends, here it
is, "Because spiritual intellect was in command, the ass was
weak. A strong rider has a lean ass! Yet because your
spiritual intellect is weak — your worn out ass has become
a dragon." — See, if with Jesus, don't have to ask where
ass is.

IDA

My ass is fine. The FBI's and CIA's, I don't know about.

EUGENE

That was a poem? Didn't rhyme.

TAYLOR

Reading is fundamental, Eugene. The scourge of illiteracy.

BILL

Da – da – dada – da – (*Seahawk music*) And that is why
the urgent need for a rite. The <u>Rite of Painting</u>. Da – da –
dada – da.

IDA

Aaaaagh!!

EUGENE

I like Ida's buttocks too. But, what was all that <u>ass</u> stuff?

Don't get it.

TAYLOR
Think of the animal. Palm Sunday. Think. Metaphor,
whatever.

KRIS
Geesh. Ida, to your issue, anyway, I'm stumped. You seem
to be up that creek without an oar.

EUGENE
Paddle, you mean.

KRIS
Who cares. Ida, think my office is the best place for you
now.

TAYLOR
(*Nods head*) Seems Ida's hit the wall of lesser men.

KRIS
Come again?

TAYLOR
They criticize what they don't understand.

IDA
You're talking about me? They?

BILL
No. No. Those in power. Where obscene righteousness
rules. Who possess narrow bigoted prejudice racist
religious ideas. And critique to make themselves feel like
masters of the subjects.

TAYLOR
Yep, and in reality, all they expose are <u>their</u> shortcomings.

IDA

Geez, glad it's not me.

BILL

(*Swings sword around and yells*) Da –da-dada-daa. Like
Lords of old, modern power snobs provide a ceaseless
source of amazement that – (*Thrusts sword in air, shouts*)
- the greater the fool, the more he is compelled to
acquaint everyone with his shortcomings. Da –da. Thus,
obscene righteousness rules in their world.

TAYLOR

I see you read Anne Perry, too. Love mysteries.

IDA

I don't. So, the government — small-minded-power-snob-
elite fools think I'm a fool and will take me down.

TAYLOR

Basically. Face it, they see the <u>Picture of Dorian Gray</u>
through a different mirror.

BILL

(*Hand on Ida's shoulder, as friends, and speaks slowly,
sympathetically*) Ida, you frighten them. Free, open
minded thinkers are feared.

EUGENE

Oh, stop the shit now. Stop this flaky gibberish and get in
step with reality.

BILL

The bane of our existence — reality. Who's? How define?
The car's or the driver's?

TAYLOR

A point, Eugene. Balzac, Becket, Joyce, Gaskell, Sands,

Rumi, Jesus, Jung, a plethora of writers have wrestled with this dilemma – reality.

KRIS

Get out. Jesus? Balzac?

EUGENE

Let me put this in terms you might appreciate.

BILL

Can't wait.

EUGENE

Think Star Wars.

BILL

Ahh. Campbell's Myth to Live By.

EUGENE

Christ!

BILL

Him too.

EUGENE

Focus. This will help. I think.

TAYLOR

(*Holds hands to ears*) OK. We're all ears.

EUGENE

Here goes. The Empire had star destroyers ---

TAYLOR

(*Breaks in*) Who's the modern Empire?

EUGENE

Big, really big, business. God, if you don't see that, can
there be hope? Anyway, well funded <u>action committees</u>
are today's star destroyers. Money being the laser beams.
Darth Vader is replaced by CEO's, who campaign fund
raise to maintain adequate weapons. And the storm
troopers are those streaming through the revolving doors of
government.

BILL

Where's Yoda?

EUGENE

<u>Dead</u>! Remember? A figment of the imagination with this
set up, where policy decisions are controlled from both
inside and outside government so the Darth whatevers
always get their way. No way "Sufi rules" like the movie
said. Business rules! Others are lemmings and better
follow obediently or it's cliff time bon voyage.

IDA

(*Sadly*) Suggesting Yoda's the false hope of the multitudes?
My salvation. Gone?

EUGENE

(*Laughs*) Funny. A creation purely spawned from
sophomorish babblings like spewed forth here. Original
man within, ha! Like there were two of everybody, for
real.

KRIS

Jesus?

EUGENE

Same. No place in business or Empire for Him either.
Except on Sundays. Or when His verbiage can be used to
advantage.

TAYLOR

It is an evil Empire.

EUGENE

No! Business! Reality. You better get with it or be lost in the void. You are my friends after all and I would not like to see that.

BILL

(*Almost whimpers*) No Yoda. No inner pressure. No soul.

EUGENE

Bingo. Yoda, the empty hologram. Not real. My advice to Ida – turn herself in and take her medicine for the good of the Empire.

IDA

What medicine? I did nothing.

EUGENE

That mob defense will not work. Telling ya.

KRIS

(*Dropped open mouth shocked*) Must man be merciless where business is concerned? Philanthropy mere vanity?

TAYLOR

Balzac concurs.

KRIS

(*Thinking*) So, the Darth Vaders are ventriloquists with government dummies on their laps, such that when could help the masses, dummy jaw flapping in reality protects big, not small, big business.

EUGENE

Now you're tasting reality. Like they purport to be for

small-government — ha — just another name for
corporate welfare queens. Thus, peasants continue
padding Big Business's bottom line.

KRIS

God. All I can think of is Norway.

EUGENE

Huh?

KRIS

Oil, a <u>natural</u> resource. In other words, belongs to <u>all</u>
people in the country. All benefit. Health. Education.
Here, belongs to a few. Billions in profit. To only the few.

TAYLOR

Seems the Empire does rule. Here.

EUGENE

So, can we eat? I'm starved.

IDA

What about me? Fool or no, does Eugene rule?

BILL

Negative vibes. So many negative vibes. (*Throws off
armor, acts disgusted*) This must stop.

EUGENE

Reality can't be avoided.

KRIS

Ida let's go. Seek sanctuary.

IDA

In a church? It would collapse.

BILL

No. No. Look. Let me demonstrate the "Ritual of
Painting." All will become clear.

*Bill goes to his easel. Prepares paints. All watch with
anticipation for some miracle. All are excited. Wide eyed.
Gather around. Bill paints and all wait.*

EUGENE

(*Finally blurts out*) What? I see nothing.

Bill just paints — all keep watching as he slings paint.

TAYLOR

(*Breaks silence*) Yes, I see. Yes. Yes. Yes. He's being
taken over by the unknown, but knowable.

EUGENE

Like shit. He's just sitting there. Painting. Wasting time.
Nothing.

KRIS

What's shit like?

EUGENE

You know what I mean.

IDA

What is war?

All stop, look at Ida, even Bill stops and looks.

ALL

Huh?

TAYLOR

(*Ignores Ida and changes subject as picks up homemade*

book. Leather cover with pages all held together with leather straps) What's this book, Bill?

                          BILL
(*Peek around canvas*) My Bible. Jefferson could do it, figured so could I.

                         EUGENE
Blasphemer.

                          BILL
Maybe. Doubt it.

                         TAYLOR
Ha. It's a bunch of quotes.

                          KRIS
His Loo 101 reading?

                           IDA
What's it say about war? My eminent imprisonment?

                         TAYLOR
(*Reading to self*) Did D.H. Lawrence really say this?

                          KRIS
What?

                         TAYLOR
Said he had to eat his own words. Thought all had been painted and could be no new work. Blaah, blaah. And that he started painting at 40. Blaah-blaah-blaah — here, wow — I quote, "Art is a form of religion minus the ten commandment business, which is sociological."

                         EUGENE
More blaspheme. A true decadent.

TAYLOR

No, an epiphany! And you need to read, Eugene, more than what critics postulate.

KRIS

Let me see that. Didn't he coin Bill's phrase "Difficult Art." (*Reads*) Hum. Listen: "The conscious delight," that's nice phraseology, "is certainly stronger in paint." Hum. Don't know what it means but sounds nice. (*Gives book back*)

IDA

Does anyone care about me?

TAYLOR

Of course Ida, you're truly our conscious delight.

KRIS

Right. We better go.

TAYLOR

(*Smiles at Ida, and goes quietly back to book*) Jung clarifies conscious delight – quote, "to make the unknown known."

EUGENE

Unless it's related to insider trading, who gives a good fuck?

KRIS

Spoken like a true empty car.

TAYLOR

Damn. Jung painted too. Said took up brush and paint — blaah-blaah — therapeutic effect — blaah-blaah. Why paint he asked, to translate emotions to images and attain inward calm and be reassured, he said.

EUGENE

Can we eat yet?

TAYLOR

Christ, listen to this, "Each time he painted he was
discovering his own <u>Myth</u>! And, get this, (*Pause*)
"as if it were a rite!"

IDA

Quick. Give me a brush. I <u>definitely</u> need a new myth.
Hurry! (*Grabs stuff to paint and does*)

EUGENE

When do you guys bring out the fiddles? I don't know if
this meal's worth it.

KRIS

Does that loo, bathroom humor, volume quote my favorite
Ar-TIST — Kandinsky.

TAYLOR

(*Shuffles through book*) Often. Like, "Artists express
thoughts, experiences, and emotions "<u>as yet unnamed</u>".
(*Said slowly*) Wow. Then suggested <u>it's</u> the only way to
answer religion's main questions.

EUGENE

Sounds like these guys ought to read a book, not just me –
<u>THE BIBLE</u>!

KRIS

(*Goes limp*) I've always wondered. At a show of his, I was
mesmerized and never felt better. Bill, you could be on to
something.

EUGENE

<u>Kris</u>! You're a lawyer. Concrete person. This is cotton

candy nothingness. Art's Nothing.

BILL

Taylor, read page 103.

TAYLOR

(*Turns pages*) This Oriental art stuff.

BILL

Ya. Just anywhere — start.

TAYLOR

Blaah-blaah oh, my. <u>Here comes Yoda</u>. Says, "The ultimate of painting's goal is to render — (*Pauses, looks up*) A <u>divine truth</u>. Not a divine truth handed out from the Gods, but one that erupted from <u>within</u> bringing mental peace."

BILL

(*Talks as paints*) Somewhere in there, Oriental artists say it's to bring forward an <u>experience</u> that had the <u>empowerment</u> of a "real" life event.

EUGENE

You guys wait here. I'll cook and serve.

IDA

(*As painting*) Are <u>we</u> artist's like alchemists then? Trying for a body that is simultaneously spirit?

EUGENE

Ida! I liked you better as a fugitive. Get real.

KRIS

He's right Ida. Big Brother never rests.

IDA

(*Painting*) Seems to me war is nothing good. Kills soldiers, civilians, destroys buildings, lives, mental health; reputations, since once start a war, <u>all</u> will do bad stuff eventually; says: might makes right. Think after 30,000 years or so could think of something better.

EUGENE

Liberal crap. Painting can't elevate your consciousness or whatever. Does nothing.

IDA

Oh, well, just an idle thought. Can I paint in jail?

EUGENE

No. But, you can lift weights.

IDA

<u>That</u> will help the psyche. Make all inmates empty cars, if ask me.

EUGENE

War's war. Necessary. Inevitable. So one best be mightiest.

TAYLOR

(*Looking through book*) Where did you find all these quotes?

BILL

(*Calls out*) Read more than one book.

TAYLOR

Tolstoy says, "— whatever happens in way of violent revolution, there will also be a private and secret revolution in man, from which a new religion will be born —" Is that what you're after Bill?

BILL

No. What we're <u>all</u> after.

EUGENE

I'm not.

KRIS

I'd have never guessed. Bet Eugene never watched grass
grow or smelled a rose.

EUGENE

(*Laughs*) Stupid. Why?

TAYLOR

Van Gogh said Oriental artists live as though they
themselves were flowers.

EUGENE

(*Just laughs loudly and shakes head*)

IDA

(*Still painting, talks idly*) To me, society is locked into a
past that's gone. Newtonian physics — gone. Assembly
line time frame — gone. Verbal intellect — not gone, but
useless here.

EUGENE

God! We're not going to start talking quantum physics
and the implications of quarks and invisible things that are
there but not, <u>are we</u>?

TAYLOR

The unknown <u>is</u> a mysterious place Eugene. Works in
mysterious ways.

IDA

Although, the brain <u>does</u> seem comfortable with Newton.

Fact: Brains don't like to be scared.

BILL
(*As paints*) Face it, the brain is under the primary control
of the powers that be: state, society and organized religion.
And responds poorly to being threatened. The more
agreement it finds, the less hormone activity, the more
secure it feels. Simple.

EUGENE
Simple, my tush (butt). You-all oughta take this act on
the road.

TAYLOR
(*Head deep in book*) Hoo! Hoo! Gauguin's art advice,
"What matters is not the things you look at, but the way
you looks at them." Damn, you gotta publish this.

KRIS
Call it — The Toilet Tao.

TAYLOR
Maybe I should order out — Chinese? God, I'm hungry.

IDA
The Ritual of Painting could be catchy, Bill. My brain is
stilled. Well, not my brain, whatever the other me is — is
calmed.

KRIS
Ida, finish up. We really should be going. Damn I sound
like her mother. (*In a high voice*) Come on kiddies we've
gotta go. Geesh.

EUGENE
So, where's the ritual? I've been patient. You're not doing
diddly.

BILL

Nothing to see. Must do.

IDA

Ya, kinda get it. Like, the brain recognizes painting as real and so is not threatened, unlike a shrink's couch, whatever, yoga, I don't know. Anyway because the physical brain is happy, it can slide sideways and neat stuff floods in —

BILL

Seen. Neat stuff seen.

IDA

Let's not get dramatic, over do it. What it floods into — don't know. Or where from.

EUGENE

(*Laughs*) Right, ha, did you see that movie "Man with two Brains." Fits. You people are nuts.

KRIS

Maybe I should partake. Yoga pretzel twisting did nothing for my brain.

BILL

See my new High Priestess for an appointment.

IDA

Me?

KRIS

God talks to you this way?

BILL

Don't know. But something's happenin.

EUGENE

Babble like that will get you put away. And I'm not
talking prison.

IDA

(*Bursts out*) <u>Hell, I'm fighting back</u>. Enough intimidation.
God, oh, <u>I'm not running</u>.

TAYLOR

I've been thinking, listening and, if you're on target, maybe
if I paint long and hard enough, push my brain way to the
head edge, maybe, just maybe, I could understand
<u>Finnigans Wake</u>. Whaddaya think Bill?

KRIS

It would take a God to understand that. Best I can do is
appreciate the words.

EUGENE

(*Yells loudly*) Enough! Enough! OK, ok you win. I'll be a
little more sensitive. OK. So stop it. You win. You could
have just said something without this elaborate hoax. I
give up. Now, let's eat. I'll be nicer.

BILL

No, Eugene. This is not about you. Can't see it? What
you see is no good, <u>must</u> do! Experience. Personalize it.
Paint!

IDA

(*Puts brushes down, looks at painting and shows all*)
Damn. Will wonders never cease? If I must.   I'm ready for
jail.

BILL

Another driver finding out they are <u>not</u> the car. Life
begins.

KRIS

Like in Joseph Campbell's <u>Personal Myths to Live By</u>.

EUGENE

(*Crys out*) <u>I need food</u>!

TAYLOR

Then after I've conquered <u>Finnegans Wake</u> I'll be ready to write my own book. The title – <u>Taylors Suit</u>.

EUGENE

What the hell? Taylor, come on now. It's late.

KRIS

Eugene, since they perused Ida's email, what about you stockbrokers? Are you all wiretapped and email scanned?

EUGENE

Say what? Christ, I'm no terrorist suspect.

IDA

Yet.

Sudden noise is heard outside the house. Hear megaphone voice say, "Please evacuate. This block must evacuate. Chemical storage plant fire in neighborhood. Evacuate now."

KRIS

Didn't know had storage depots in residential areas. Not here anyway.

IDA

Maybe just want to search the houses.

EUGENE

Don't be daft. They'd need a warrant.

KRIS

Not now, if not at home. Patriot Act.

EUGENE

What good are lawyers?

KRIS

Lawyers?

BILL

Let's go, folks.

All dash out the door and it is quiet, for short time. Stage is empty of people. Then rocking chair starts moving some, lights on and off, book moves and other acts maybe (holograms) to indicate stage not empty.

KRIS

(*Voice more ethereal*) Thank God for these vacation times.

TAYLOR

(*Voice ethereal*) For sure. It's great getting out of their bodies for awhile. That autopilot gene was a great idea. Praise evolution.

EUGENE

(*Voice ethereal*) Be nice if we could get these periods to last longer. We don't get out enough. Stretch our souls. Relax.

IDA

(*Voice ethereal*) My bunions still hurt. How's that work? She has them, I feel them. No justice.

BILL

(*Voice ethereal*) Aches and pains, that's all we get from

them. Holy halos, think they'll ever realize they're us and not them?

TAYLOR
(*Voice ethereal*) In your reality. How stupid! We're just dreams to them, when we try to communicate. Why can't they see?

KRIS
(*Voice ethereal*) And we're a whole sight better and faster than their stupid computer things. Machines. How archaic.

BILL
(*Voice ethereal*) Us, do you believe it, give names to us like visualization, dreams, id. God knows what else we're called.

IDA
(*Voice ethereal*) Anything but <u>them</u>. Us <u>is</u> them. God give me strength. Souls — us!

EUGENE
(*Voice ethereal*) I blame it on that Cro-Magnum infection, millenniums ago. It <u>was</u> powerful. Lord knows.

IDA
(*Voice ethereal*) Right on. But, <u>that</u> powerful! Who would of thunk? Greed, selfishness, nastiness would be so lasting.

EUGENE
(*Voice ethereal*) Too bad it left that mark on their genes to be passed on and on and on. They need to overcome it. Desperately. Yet, don't even recognize the problem exists.

IDA

(*Voice ethereal*) Probably would have been better off with
that dinosaur man.

EUGENE

(*Voice ethereal*) Got that right. <u>A</u>men.

TAYLOR

(*Voice ethereal*) Let's be serious. What can we do? Do
you ever think humans will get the dualism thing? Or the
point of life? Jesus stuff?

IDA

(*Voice ethereal*) No. And no. None. Some maybe.
Aaah! We're doomed to purgatory.

BILL

(*Voice ethereal*) Do we start all over?

KRIS

(*Voice ethereal*) God, I hate to ponder that. The years.
Millions, wasn't it?

TAYLOR

(*Voice ethereal*) Their bodies sure are poorly designed
pieces of transitory baggage.

EUGENE

(*Voice ethereal*) Or as they would say – crap.

KRIS

(*Voice ethereal*) What is crap? Don't get it.

BILL

(*Voice ethereal*) Don't ask. A physical thing.

TAYLOR

(*Voice ethereal*) Wish mine would lose some weight. Eat better. Those extra trace minerals are murder.

BILL

(*Voice ethereal*) Thought they almost fathomed the car analogy. Seems we'll never get more than just close.

TAYLOR

(*Voice ethereal*) They <u>are</u> a frightened species. Without doubt, a real handicap.

KRIS

(*Voice ethereal*) God does work in mysterious ways.

EUGENE

(*Voice ethereal*) Ya, but heaven it all, couldn't He have done better? This may be too much to overcome.

BILL

(*Voice ethereal*) I hear them returning. Remember, "<u>group think</u>" – souls are <u>all</u>. Physical – inconsequential.

IDA

(*Voice ethereal*) That's tough. They don't even know souls exist, let alone souls need educated, nurtured. Or that all souls are one.

KRIS

(*Voice ethereal*) Or that <u>it's primary</u>! It's hopeless. And war's an oxymoron.

EUGENE

(*Voice ethereal*) Shit. Shit. (Say several shits quieter and quieter)

Door bangs open, all come in.

KRIS

Whoo. It's cold in here all of a sudden.

IDA

Did you feel that? Gave me a sudden shiver.

BILL

Ya, like a cold wind just blew into my bones.

TAYLOR

Or like walked over someone's grave.

EUGENE

Can we eat?

Stage darkens, slide is shown of a Jung quote.

CARL JUNG

But what is the difference between a real illusion and a
healing religions experience? It is merely a difference in
words. --- nobody can know what the ultimate things are.
We must, therefore, take them as we experience them.
And if such experiences helps to make your life healthier,
more beautiful, more complete to those you love, you may
safely say: This was the grace of God.

CURTAIN FALLS

www.ingramcontent.com/pod-product-compliance
Lightning Source LLC
Chambersburg PA
CBHW031606260626
47154CB00020B/1641